The Panther Moon

by

Beth Trissel

The Secret Warrior Series

This is a work of fiction. Names, characters, places, and incidents are either the product of the author's imagination or are used fictitiously, and any resemblance to actual persons living or dead, business establishments, events, or locales, is entirely coincidental.

The Panther Moon

Cover Art by *Debbie Taylor*

The Wild Rose Press, Inc.
PO Box 708
Adams Basin, NY 14410-0708
Visit us at www.thewildrosepress.com

Publishing History
First New Adult Edition, 2016
Print ISBN 978-1-5092-0996-5
Digital ISBN 978-1-5092-0997-2

The Secret Warrior Series
Published in the United States of America

One after the other, coyote shifters
took shape around her and Jimmy. A whirl, and there
they were—appearing without sound, camouflaged like
chameleons. Not a wolf trick she'd mastered. Maybe
she should. Fast. The devils slunk closer.

Corn silk hair like Eve's blew in the stiff breezes,
and various shades of red and brown. Males and
females sported loose lengths flapping in the wind,
dreadlocks, ponytails, and shaved heads. There must
have been at least a dozen sinewy forms, dressed in
earthen tones or shadowy black.

Cunning eyes fixed on Morgan, barely giving
Jimmy a glance. Emboldened men and lean, mean
women stalked nearer, their coyote musk obnoxious to
her wolf self. They weren't armed. 'Go for the throat'
must be their attack mode.

Should she shift? Only partly. A wolf couldn't use
weapons or catch the next vortex. Not that she'd swirl
away and leave Jimmy behind. Besides the need to
protect him, she was a warrior. Her duty lay in
defending Wapicoli territory.

How stupid to let herself get trapped in the first
place! Hadn't Jackson warned her a lone wolf was a
dead wolf?

Dedication

To my dear niece Sara,
whose enthusiasm helped me craft this story.

Chapter One
Riding the Wind

November, the Virginia Mountains

"Whooohoooo!" Arms upraised, Morgan swirled round and round like an ice-skater in the mini whirlwind. Fallen leaves snatched up by the bluster spun alongside her.

Wild. Wonderful. Free.

Kid brother Jimmy watched from the large stone he'd hunkered on. "You're not *The Last Airbender*, but awesome!"

"Kind've like *Korra*? Sweet." She touched down and immediately sprang into another vortex fast-taking shape.

Heady with exhilaration, she lifted off the ground. Spongy moss, tawny fern, and the remains of October's splendor carpeted the floor beneath her. "Jimmy, look!"

"Holy flying cow, Batgirl!"

The very breath of the forest filled her dizzying senses. She inhaled the rich aroma of crumbling earth, living plants, and the mingled scent of the creatures that made their homes here, the essence of life in these mountains. Crimson berries and gold glints brightened the rusts dominant in the woods rippling around her. Brilliant blue sky peeked between the bare branches and evergreen boughs tossing overhead.

Pale yellow hair whipped across her face. The cold cut through her leather coat and pants, but she didn't care. She was harnessing the elements. First fire. Now air!

He swept his hands at the sky. "Wait until I get Egbert trained. Then I'll soar!"

She envisioned him riding his thunderbird above the clouds. "You'll rule!"

A scolding blue jay streaked by, its vivid feathers catching the afternoon light. Startled squirrels scampered up a lichen encrusted trunk, chattering in protest. White-tailed deer jerked up their heads and bounded away on slender legs. Loudest of all were the raucous crows. Their black wings flapped heavenward, inky smudges in the sky. She'd caused quite a stir.

Euphoria bubbled inside her. What care had she for the animals' alarm amid such harmless glory? Each thrilling revolution lasted only seconds. She eagerly leapt into the next leafy spiral.

How high could she go?

How fast?

Focusing all her mental abilities on levitation, she circled above Jimmy.

He jumped up to tag her boots. His gloved fingers barely brushed the soles. "We should get you a cape. You're freakin' *Supergirl*."

She laughed, reveling in her triumph. The fur coat Miriam had made him from a vintage relic she'd cut down, 'to keep the dear boy warm' gave him the appearance of a fuzzy rabbit. The good woman might as well have added ears to the hood. "And you're a big bunny!"

"With glasses. Not the look I was shooting for.

Miriam was fresh out of Elven cloaks."

"Imagine that." She wheeled ecstatically. "I could do this all day!"

"No, you can't." He hopped off the stone, the bow, quiver of arrows, and supply pouch hanging by straps over his pint-sized shoulders. "Earth to Morgan. We're supposed to meet Jackson and Hawth—"

"At the Divining Tree," she finished for him. "I know."

The giant oak, bent to one side and struck by lightning multiple times, had survived not only those trials but untold centuries. Civilizations had come and gone and it remained, a sentinel to the ages. One massive limb pointed toward the small clearing in the woods where the mysterious Chief Okema had said the Star People landed over two hundred years ago. He'd notched the surrounding trunks with the sign of an arrow to signify the site, and the Wapicoli kept the grassy spot free of overgrowth for the space aliens' prophesied return.

Not only the oak's vast age, but the energy flowing from it accounted for the noble title. The deep-rooted tree tapped into the ancient wisdom of the forest. Those who stood beneath the immense canopy and laid their hands on the fissured bark might gain unique insight, if they were deemed worthy. A reward rarely bestowed, about once every hundred years.

So sacred was the site, Okema had only recently revealed it to her and Jimmy. Now, the woodland sanctuary was the favored meeting place for her, Jimmy, Jackson, and his cousin, Hawthorn. Dilly wasn't yet initiated. The ditzy girl didn't even realize she was a witch, and her infamous mama a lizard shifting crone.

"They'll wonder where we are," Jimmy reminded her, like trying to gain the attention of someone high on pixie dust.

The guys had gone ahead while she and Jimmy were delayed with Miriam fussing over the coat. Archery practice and yet more warrior training was planned for the afternoon. She'd gladly put off the drill, except for hanging out with Jackson. Alone time together was as challenging to come by as the blessing from the Divining Tree.

"Give me a sec, Batboy. This spot's perfect for dust devils, and I've only just learned how to ride them."

He shook his furry head. "My sister the superhero. Who knew?"

"Timing's the key. Tricky to judge." She vaulted into the center of a spiral the instant a new one formed. But speed ranked among her newly acquired wolf skills, and the power that came with being the Seventh Morcant.

Whirling breathlessly, she rose even higher. No wolf girl had ever done this before. She'd bet no Wapicoli had either, except Okema. His abilities were beyond her understanding.

Jimmy raised his hand in a salute. "All hail. I declare you a true *Airbender*."

The supreme tribute from the whiz kid.

"You've got this down, Morgan. Time to dock on the landing pad."

"Oh, okay." Trees closed in. She pushed away from the trunk with her toes and sailed to Jimmy. Leaves crunched underfoot as she settled beside him.

He gestured at the sun-dappled trail. Branches, underbrush, and twists in the path obscured the track winding ahead of them. "Try swirling your way to our rendezvous."

"There's a thought. Maybe I—" 'Could' remained on the tip of her tongue.

One sniff of the cloying sweetness of gardenia and she pivoted nearly face-to-face with Eve. The coyote witch was only yards away. She used the floral perfume to mask her animal musk, but gardenias didn't bloom in these woods. *Odeur* of skunk would better suit her.

Fury surged through Morgan at the jolt Eve gave her. That girl had some nerve! How had she appeared so suddenly? Her tan leggings, brown boots, and buckskin jacket blended well with the forest, but Morgan should've detected her sooner. Where had she come from? Was she part Pantera, taking shape out of thin air?

Come to think of it, Jackson had said coyote shifters were sneaky. *No kidding.*

She eyed the intruder with all the affection she'd direct at a rattlesnake and grasped the hilt of the sheathed knife at her waist. Six revolutions and she could sink the blade in her chest. "What do you want?"

Eve's cold blue gaze pierced her. If possible, those eyes were even chillier than 'the ice queen's' as Morgan had dubbed her inner wolf. "I've come to see Dilly."

Their last encounter hadn't left Morgan with the warm fuzzies. "You treat Dilly like trash. Why should she want to see you?"

"Because we're sisters," Eve hissed.

"Barely. I'll give her your fond regards. She can

return your visit if she likes. Can't think why she would." Nor was Morgan about to let her. Eve and her demon-lizard mother had probably discovered Dilly's *gifts* and plotted to use the gullible girl for their devious purposes.

Defiance lit Eve's stare, and she waved her aside with a perfectly manicured hand. "This isn't a request. I'm going to see my sister."

Morgan knew her own eyes were changing to white-hot blue. "Okema will never allow you to reach the lodge."

A secretive and incredibly annoying smile curved Eve's pink lips. "I'm already closing in."

The lodge was about two miles away, as the crow flies. It was true, Okema's protective circle should extend this far. Now and then gaps formed in the barrier, and he reinforced it. Were his powers waning even more than she realized?

Unnerving to contemplate, but she didn't flinch. "Let's put it this way. You're not getting past me."

Again, the maddening smirk. "You think I came alone?"

Morgan gritted her teeth. Of course she hadn't.

One after the other, coyote shifters took shape around her and Jimmy. A whirl, and there they were— appearing without sound, camouflaged like chameleons. Not a wolf trick she'd mastered. Maybe she should. Fast. The devils slunk closer.

Corn silk hair like Eve's blew in the stiff breezes, and various shades of red and brown. Males and females sported loose lengths flapping in the wind, dreadlocks, ponytails, and shaved heads. There must have been at least a dozen sinewy forms, dressed in earthen tones or shadowy black.

Cunning eyes fixed on Morgan, barely giving Jimmy a glance. Emboldened men and lean, mean women stalked nearer, their coyote musk obnoxious to her wolf self. They weren't armed. 'Go for the throat' must be their attack mode.

Should she shift? Only partly. A wolf couldn't use weapons or catch the next vortex. Not that she'd swirl away and leave Jimmy behind. Besides the need to protect him, she was a warrior. Her duty lay in defending Wapicoli territory.

How stupid to let herself get trapped in the first place! Hadn't Jackson warned her a lone wolf was a dead wolf?

Click. The flame of a lighter caught her notice. Then smoky sizzle. Out of the corner of her eye, she saw the ever-ready Jimmy toss a sparkler a short distance from where they stood. He dipped back into his pack amid startled glances. Out came the duct tape. He bound a second sparkler on the side of an arrow in an instant. A rip of the tape with his teeth, flick of the lighter, and he shot it blazing into the sky. The signal for backup. His superpower lay in quick thinking, and he'd caught the trespassers off-guard.

Howls rose from the surrounding ridges. Wapicoli were answering his summons, but it would take minutes not seconds before the first wolves reached them. She and Jimmy had moments. If she distracted the pack, maybe he could get away.

She wasn't exactly helpless. Not by a long shot.

Opening her balled fists, she flashed her fingers at Eve in a fiery blue current. The alpha leader tumbled to the ground. They'd played this game before. Did Eve want more? Morgan would gladly bring it.

Angry snarls tore from the feral pack. Some were shifting. Coyotes in animal and human form lunged at her.

Time to use the wind. She leapt into a fast forming spout. Drawing on her powers, she blasted fiery energy at them as she wheeled in sizzling revolutions. The air crackled bluish white and smelled like the earth after a lightning strike. Coyotes fell back on each side of her. They were only down temporarily, unless she'd knocked them senseless, but it was satisfying to see them careen in every direction.

The funnel dissipated, and she stopped spinning. "Go!" she cried, waving at Jimmy to run.

"No way!" He shot an arrow at the ripped male scrambling to his feet, dreadlocks bouncing. The would-be attacker jerked the sharp missile from his bloody shoulder with a howl. Batboy had winged him.

Taking flight in another wind spout, she zapped his comrades struggling to rise. Glory hallelujah! She was on fire!

She knew from experience, though, her use of blue energy was draining. Better save some for later and fight wolf style.

Eve came to life. Venom creased her pale beauty. Shifting to half-wolf, Morgan sprang. Their eyes met as she knocked her flat.

Weird vibes in that frozen blue gaze. Not the hypnotic mind control she'd battled with the gorgon-like mother, but something was definitely off. Badmojo.

Recoiling from Eve, she did a backflip, kicked out, and sent a hard muscled on comer flying. The skinhead slammed to the ground. A recovering female rushed at her. She spun on her heels, kicking and ducking. The second coyote skidded to her knees.

Tenacious bunch. Why didn't they flee?

Eve hurtled at her. A Morcant female, especially the seventh, was stronger than this pack queen—than any of them. She struck without hesitation, clipping Eve's perfect jaw. A fist thrust in the coyote shifter's midriff, a forceful shove, and she face-planted in the leafy earth. Morgan could've crowed.

Jimmy didn't waver either. Dodging on comers, he kept up a barrage of arrows, zinging them off nearly as fast as Jackson. Coyotes were forced to take cover behind trees. Those darting from trunk to trunk risked an arrow in the leg or arm. He wasn't shooting to kill. Yet.

Did nothing keep Eve down? She turned onto her side and nailed Morgan with the full force of those eyes.

What the heck? She was strangely unable to move and struggled as if caught in quicksand. Black magic. It had to be. "Jimmy!" Her mouth still worked.

"Gotcha!" Rather than big sister saving him, the kid poised with an arrow on the string in her defense. Swiveling to the left and right, he threatened aggressors tempted to step from behind the trunks.

Eve wasted no time, either. With a flick of her pink fingernails, she manipulated a tangle of grape vines winding through the trees. The wooden tendrils snaked around Morgan and pinned both arms to her sides.

Holy crap! She was trapped. *Impossible*. But she couldn't move.

She summoned her inner blue light. The vines should explode into pieces.

9

They didn't.

Her reserves must be more depleted than she knew, or Eve possessed greater power than she realized. With her hands immobilized, she couldn't rub the energy-giving moonstone at her throat.

Wearing the most irritating smile in this world, Eve stepped toward her. Jimmy took aim. "Get back, witch!"

Another tangle of vines whirled at him. And paused in mid-air. Eve whipped her hand at them again. The vines halted as if stopped by unseen fingers and fell at his feet.

"What the?" Her exultant leer changed to puzzled anger.

Then Morgan understood the delay with the coat, the small bundles of herbs Miriam had tucked in the pockets, the scented water she'd sprinkled on the fur, and the murmured incantation. A protection spell.

"You can't harm him," she informed little miss high and mighty.

"He can't shoot us all before we get *you*," Eve sneered. "Now!"

The onrush was instantaneous. Coyotes in human and animal form hurled themselves at her and Jimmy. He was bowled over in the crush. The coat didn't keep him from hitting the forest floor and rolling. At least, it cushioned his fall.

Gotta get loose! Morgan wrenched against the vines.

Not smart. They gripped her more tightly. It was only a matter of time before her power resurged. But how long?

Eve paused in front of her, the revolting stench

more pungent than ever. She itched to smack the simper from her face but would settle for snapping her thin arms, or neck.

"Before we cut your throat, I'll take this." Eve reached for the moonstone. "Don't want it bloodied."

Pulsing light shot from the orb, and it glowed with the radiance of the aurora borealis. Pink, green, yellow, blue, and violet rays shone in a mini Northern Lights display.

Was that a faint hum? Good heavens—the stone.

Eve snatched back her hand, staring in disbelief. Surrounding coyotes faltered. All were riveted on the sight. So was Morgan. The gem had never done this before. Was the mystical gift reacting to Eve's sinister magic, or anyone who tried to steal it? And what was with the humming?

Jimmy didn't hesitate. Taking advantage of the momentary shock, he regained his stance, an arrow on the string. He pointed it at Eve. "No matter who comes at my sister next, I'm shooting you. And it won't be in the shoulder!"

"Aim for the heart, Jimbo! If she's got one!" shouted a familiar voice.

Jackson! *Thank God*. His beloved scent wafted on the wind. Relief like flood waters swelled in Morgan.

He raced to her in a blur of snarling, snapping wolves. His long black hair blew in the gusts. "Love to stay and chat," he called after the scattering coyotes. "But Mateo's coming!"

An image of the Pantera gang leader appeared in her mind. Those murderous tawny eyes, the hue of an inferno when they changed. God help them. The devil himself was back.

11

Panteras and coyotes were no allies. Eve departed in a whirl, apparently how she and her kind traveled.

A frown on his handsome face, Jackson tore at the vines ensnaring Morgan with strong arms. The open leather jacket he wore revealed muscles rippling beneath his white Henley shirt. "I didn't realize she was capable of this."

"I sensed it. Should have been more cautious. And not wasted my power playing around." She could kick herself.

Jimmy hauled at the tendrils. "Learning to fly's handy."

"Heck yeah," Jackson grunted.

"So far, only when there's wind," she clarified.

"It's a start." He wrenched the final tangle from her ankles while the wolves sniffed for any lingering coyotes. Among her rescuers were Hawthorne and Roan Wapicoli.

She tested her arms and legs. Back to normal. "The spell must've broken with Eve's departure."

"An arrow through her heart would probably have a similar effect," Jimmy muttered.

"What about Mateo?" Dread thudded in Morgan's chest. "Do we fight him? I really could use time to recharge."

"Not now." Jackson grabbed her hand. "Back to the lodge! All of you! Something's not right with Okema," he added under his breath. "No one should be making it this close to home."

Realization sank in. "The protective circle's broken?"

His eyes met hers, grim awareness in their dark depths. "I fear so."

Chapter Two
Protect the Pack

Clouds blotted out the sun. The shadowed trees shook with less force, and the dust devils disappeared. Hawthorne, Roan, and the other guys still in wolf form after racing to Morgan's aid bounded in front of her and Jackson. They'd reach the lodge first and carry warning to Miriam, if she needed it. Likely, the wise woman knew more than they did.

Even without shifting, Morgan and Jackson could streak ahead of any human. They mustn't outrun Jimmy, though. No one should be alone in these woods now.

Batboy trotted at their heels, muffling the crunch of leaves. The whiz kid was naturally adept. She quieted her footfall, and Jackson was super silent, part of the Native American/wolf thing.

"Where did you see Mateo?" She kept her voice down in case the demon cat was within hearing range.

"Didn't," he grunted. "Roan and his brother, Sam, were bow hunting when they spotted him and half a dozen or more of his gang setting up camp, way too close for comfort. They snuck away and found Hawth and me about the time Jimbo sent up the signal. Smart move, dude."

"Thanks," Jimmy huffed from behind.

"Yeah." Her stomach churned. "Too many enemies

on the prowl in Wapicoli territory."

Jackson's grave demeanor wasn't encouraging. "And they're growing in strength and number. Add coyotes and their witch queen to the list."

Her conscience needled her. "That's one enemy I maybe shouldn't have made."

He waved aside her regret. "Would've happened anyway. Wapicoli and coyotes don't get on. Particularly the alphas."

If the red-hot irritation every time she saw Eve was any indication, Morgan agreed. She hated to ask her next question, but must. "Do you think something's happened to Okema?"

For a long moment, he was quiet. "Okema's not himself. We've got to find out what's going on and plan our strategy. There's more of *them* than there are of us."

A sobering prospect. "Guess I didn't fully realize how dependent we are on him."

"I did." His short reply said it all.

"You've both got power, too," Jimmy interjected. "Heaps, if you tap into it. Morgan's learning fast."

Jackson angled his face at her in a wistful half smile. "Okema knew you would. That's why he summoned you to us. I just want to be a *normal* werewolf, warrior, Star Person descendant."

"Destined to be the next chief and take his place," she prompted.

"Apart from that." He wore his reluctance like a mantle.

"Real normal," Jimmy quipped. "Lots of those around, mighty leader."

"At least you guys had a taste of ordinary—"

"While on the run, watching our backs. But kind

of," she finished for him. "I mean, we went to school and watched Saturday morning cartoons. Slept in sometimes."

He flung up a hand. "Exactly. Is that so much to ask?"

"With the fate of the Wapicoli hinging on us? A bit. But I get what you're saying. I want that too." *And him.*

Jimmy quickened his pace to keep up with Jackson's ground-covering strides. "Face it, *Supergirl*, and star person descendent/warrior/ werewolf dude. Ordinary sailed at your birth."

Unarguably. It didn't deter her from wanting to curl up before the hearth with Jackson and let this rabbit-hole world turn without them for a while.

"When the going gets tough, the tough don't whine about missing *Sponge Bob*," Jimmy wore on.

"I didn't," Jackson shot back. "But it would be nice to have a choice in how I live my life."

"We always have a choice. If we accept the outcome." Jimmy sounded like a mini adult; a pious one.

Jackson narrowed his eyes. "I swear if you don't stop lecturing me, Jimbo, I'm gonna leave you in the dust."

"I'd probably be fine. Keenest wits in dogdom."

"And he's wearing a charmed coat," Morgan inserted into the exchange. "Did you know?"

"No, but I can guess from whom. We're gonna need Grandma Miriam."

Like a flutter of wings, hope stirred inside her. "Maybe we should reconvene the fellowship, too."

Somber awareness had cooled Jackson's

annoyance. "If Okema's out of commission, we'll need all the help we can get."

"Time to blow Queen Susan's horn, and wherever you are, help will come to you." Batboy referred to the magical horn from *The Chronicles of Narnia*.

Jackson waved him on. "I'll leave that particular quest in your capable hands, Jimbo. The first task of any leader is to delegate."

"You're already alpha of our pack," Morgan reasoned, trying to instill confidence.

"Yeah. But not of the whole freaking clan. Seriously, I'm giving Rafe and Mato a call."

She nodded. "What about Joe and your Uncle Ray?"

"Them too, if they can spare the time away from the store and the band. We've gotta circle the wagons."

"I thought that's what pioneers did when Indians attacked?" She gestured at the trio. "*We're* the warriors."

"True, and we will fight. Probably to the death. First, we have to shore up our defenses against Panteras, coyotes, your crazed uncle and his enemy werewolf pack," Jackson muttered. "Did I miss anyone? Oh, right. The Mongol horde."

She eyed him blankly. "That hardcore English punk band?"

Jimmy snorted. "History's not her strong point. He means Genghis Khan. Heard of that ruthless killer?"

"Yeah. Him I've heard of. He and Mateo would get along great, until one killed the other and took over their empire."

Jackson considered her in the studied way he had. "If we're lucky, maybe someone will knock off Mateo."

Morgan suspected that someone was her. And Jackson, when he stopped resenting his birthright and claimed it.

Chapter Three
Secret Warrior

Now what? Not date night. That's for sure.

Morgan sat by Jackson among the uneasy band gathered in the main room of the lodge 'to take stock of our situation,' as Miriam termed it earlier at the supper table, with sage nods from Peter and Buck. Willow and Aunt M. had also agreed. So far, only the usual foursome and Dilly were present.

After a hurried meal, Roan and Sam had hastened away to sound the alarm to other Wapicoli. Word would quickly spread through nearby ridges. Okema was gone. This much was certain.

Where?

No one knew.

Dread mixed with the emptiness in Morgan's gut, emotions she'd never expected to experience at Okema's sudden removal. He'd cursed her family and should be her enemy, but he'd become an unlikely mentor and a psychic bond linked them.

Too weird for words.

Stifling a sigh, she ran her critical gaze over the familiar room. Everything looked the same. Decorations from the recent Halloween party remained, minus the multitude of pumpkins. Garlands of preserved fall leaves accented with acorns and bittersweet berries entwined the rafters, trailing down the log walls. Colorful bunches of Indian corn tied with twine added to the autumnal flavor. Her surroundings smelled the same, a meld of wood smoke and herbs. But nothing was right.

Carvings of wolves embellished the wide mantel above Batboy, who sat cross-legged before the blazing hearth with Egbert. The infant thunderbird roosted on a wooden block beside Jimmy, too big to perch on the leather gauntlet shielding his arm from the talons, sharp even now. He resembled a cross between an oversized goose and a plump eagle with fuzzy gray feathers. The Native American version of a baby dragon. He couldn't fly yet but fluttered his wings. The cord attached to his ankle kept him tethered to the block.

Jimmy tossed the probing beak a frozen mouse pellet. "Maybe the Star People fetched Okema while we were off."

Hugging Jackson's warmth, Morgan pressed near him on the handcrafted leather couch. "I figured they'd stay long enough to say howdy, or whatever they do."

"And make more of an entrance after all these years," Hawthorne added. He'd positioned himself on his cousin's other side with Dilly huddled beside him. "Glowing lights, whirling space ship, that sort of thing."

"Yeah. I can't wrap my mind around Okema's absence." He was the epicenter of this bizarre world she'd embraced.

"Me either." Jackson brooded into the fire, his gold-tinged eyes glinting. His inflamed mood had caused them to turn slightly. He'd left his hair loose, and the flames played over his face. He looked hotter than hot, but romance was likely the last thing on his mind.

"I expected a goodbye and some last minute instructions before takeoff, at the least," he said through tight lips.

"Maybe he's gone walkabout." Hawth was rarely serious, as the mirth hinting in his hazel eyes proclaimed.

"Do chiefs like him go off that way?" His joke was lost on Dilly.

"There are no chiefs like Okema." Jackson shouldered back against the couch, arms crossed at his chest, mouth clamped.

Morgan knew what he was thinking. What were they gonna do without Okema? What if his absence was permanent? And why had he gone? Seriously.

Having the protective circle down was bad enough. They were fortunate Miriam had shielded the lodge with a spell. It carried no further than the yard, though, she'd said, and would last only a few days until the process must be repeated.

"What if Okema's been kidnapped?" Worry hazed Dilly's blue-green eyes, accented with smoky liner.

Jackson groaned under his breath. "He's far too powerful for that. Whatever's happened, it appears we're on our own for the foreseeable future. And at war with nearly everybody."

Jimmy tossed Egbert another pellet. "Better call this the war room if we'll be planning battle strategy in here."

"We're gonna need maps." Hawthorne wagged a finger at the log walls. "War rooms always have them pinned up."

"And a lot more people present, if you're picturing

WWII movies." Jackson swiveled his head toward the door. "Where is everyone?"

"If you mean the elders?" Hawth shrugged. "We were told to come, so here we are like good little warriors."

Dilly tossed her long auburn hair. "I'm not a warrior."

"No, you have other talents." He wasn't referring to her cooking. Passable, at best. Or her kissing. Awesome, no doubt.

About time someone told her the truth.

"I'm sure glad Rafe and Mato can come," Jackson muttered. "If this is the support we can expect."

"Roger that." Jimmy fed the insatiable bird another nugget. He'd set a lot of mouse traps to stock his inventory.

Pretty gross, but Egbert had to eat. Soon he'd be large enough to consume rabbits. Such a potentially aggressive creature must be well-tended, trained, and on their side. He'd bonded with Batboy. The resident owl regarded the pair from the rafters above, bobbing his head for a better look.

Dilly chewed her lower lip, slicked with gloss. "What if Okema's dead?"

Morgan feared the same thing but hadn't verbalized it aloud. Plus, wouldn't she sense his passing?

"He can't be dead." Jackson was absolute in his reply. "Because I'm not yet Kitch Wabi Ayapia, The Great White Wolf. My Shawnee name, and my destiny."

"Of course." She remembered now. He wouldn't completely come into his own until Okema's time on

21

earth was finished.

The group seemed a little heartened by his assurance.

"Okema's out there somewhere. Meanwhile, I'm the next supreme alpha. He's made that clear enough." Jackson ran his narrow gaze around the assembly. "Okay then. Jimbo, continue training Egbert and work with Hawth to invent something diabolical we can use in battle. Morgan, practice levitating without the wind. Dilly, you're a witch, by the way. Use your powers for good and for us. Your sister's a coyote shifting she-devil, and you know your mom's a demon lizard, right?"

Mouth open, Dilly gaped at him, as did the rest of them.

He laced his hands behind his head. "Great. We're all up to speed."

It wasn't like him to be so brusque. He must be hurting big time. Morgan studied him closely. "While we're doing our assigned tasks, what will you do?"

His eyes were slits. "Figure out where Okema's gone."

"Maybe he doesn't wish to be found," Miriam suggested, silently entering the room. "Perhaps he needs rest. Maintaining the circle is draining. He grows old. He's near the end of his seventh lifetime."

"Not *that* old," Jackson argued. "He's still plenty powerful. Or was, just days ago at the party."

"The confrontation with Morgan's uncle and the renegade werewolves may have taken more from him than we realize."

Chin thrust out, Jackson clenched his fists at his sides. "I can't take Okema's place. I can't *be* him."

"No one expects you to, nor are you yet fully equipped for this great task," Miriam soothed, her voice a balm. "But you must lead to the best of your ability. He entrusted the clan to you."

Jackson bowed his head with the heaviness of this undeniable charge. "I will do as I must."

The weight of his burden glistened in Miriam's brown eyes. "You will do well."

Pausing before the hearth, she sat in a chair made of vines and bent twigs, far enough from Egbert so her long skirt wouldn't be nibbled. Silver hair fell over the blue shawl wrapped around her slender shoulders. Angling the chair toward the gathering, she surveyed them. The glass beads in her feathered earrings flashed in the firelight.

Her liquid gaze traveled each face. "You are not alone. I am here. More shall come. And you are far more powerful than you know." She lingered on Jackson's troubled countenance. "Okema will return...I cannot say when. Meanwhile, I shall help you lead."

She was the obvious choice. Not his father, or Uncle Buck—Hawthorne's dad. This extraordinary woman.

The gifted healer cocked her head at Morgan. "What is that hum?"

It had grown so faint, she'd nearly forgotten, and Jackson was probably too preoccupied to inquire. "Oh. My moonstone came to glowing life and hummed, far louder than this, earlier today when Eve tried to snatch it from me."

Dilly jerked as if stung by a bee. "You saw her?"

"Sure did. And her sneaky pack. They're looking for you." She waved the shocked girl aside

23

momentarily, and continued. "I don't know why the stone's doing this."

Miriam's eyes brimmed with insight. "The question isn't only why, but *who*?"

"What do you mean?"

"Who is it contacting?" she asked softly.

Lordy, Morgan gulped.

Jackson turned to stare at her. All eyes in the room were fixed on her, even Egbert's. And the bobbing owl overhead.

Miriam widened her arms to embrace the heavens. "It's a gift from the Star People, first to your Grandma Sarah, and now you."

Jimmy squirmed in excitement. "E.T. is phoning home."

"I was gonna say that!" Hawthorne pounced.

"Too late. I called it." Batboy was smug.

While they argued over who snagged the punch line, she tried to fathom her necklace acting as a homing beacon to some distant galaxy. Cue the 'wonder music' from *Interstellar*.

"Did Eve activate the signal, or would it have done that anyway?"

"I cannot say. This is unexpected," Miriam said.

"Like anything else today has gone as planned?" Jackson tossed back.

Morgan totally got why he was hurt and brooding, but he wasn't himself. And he definitely wasn't approachable. He'd shut himself off, and she needed him close.

Dilly raised her hand like a kid in school. "What does Eve and her pack want with me?"

"Another good question. Whatever it is, I wouldn't

trust her." Miriam spoke for them all.

Chapter Four
Sir Jackson

"You can bring one? Awesome!" Phone to his ear, Jimmy leapt up and down on the bench across from Morgan at the breakfast table.

Startled by his early morning exuberance, she sloshed her coffee. "Cripes, Jimmy."

The psyched kid waved her aside. "See ya," he said, ending the call. "Yaaasssssss! Rafe and Mato are on it. He returned the burner phone to Jackson, seated beside him. Eyes twinkling like Santa's elf, he angled a grin at Hawthorne. "Admit it. You wish you'd thought of it first."

A smile tugged at Hawthorne's lips, and a nod accompanied his shrug. "This could work, Cubbie."

"Kayoed!" Arms crossed over Hawth's hand-me-down *Iron Man* sweatshirt reaching nearly to his knees, Jimmy took a bow.

Amusement lightened Jackson's gaze. If anyone could cheer him up, it was the kid; it sure as heck hadn't been Morgan. Still no tender glances or soft words from Jackson for her.

He high-fived the boy bouncing on his seat. "You're hyped. I didn't expect action this fast."

Supreme satisfaction etched Batboy's freckled face. "Well, our enemies are fast. So are you guys—" He gestured at the usual circle, plus Aunt Maggie, tucked around the table with them. Miriam and Willow paused in their kitchen bustle to listen. "But this'll give us an edge. I'll mark all incoming with the paintball gun. The model Mato and Rafe are bringing has a red dot reflex site scope and a manual from the US freakin' Army. The balls are glow-in-the-dark. You can easily spot who's been hit, night or day. See them coming and hunt them down if they get away. Tag and bag."

Lines creased Dilly's smooth forehead. "Don't you have to be a really good shot not to miss?"

The pint-sized marksman exuded confidence. "Think I've got this covered. I'll practice, of course."

Jimmy was the can-do kid. Now that caffeine was firing up Morgan's brain cells, his paintball scheme made sense. Judging by Dilly's furrowed brow, she remained skeptical.

"You'll probably only get one try. After that..." The girl's uncertainty heightened the concern in Aunt M.'s blue gaze.

She wore the haunted look of one who wished she'd done more to protect him and still longed to scoop him under her wings. "You'll be careful, won't you?"

He raised his hand in the two-fingered Cub Scout pledge. "Safety first. I'll hide behind trees, conduct sneak attacks."

"As much as he can, anyway." Morgan waved her spoon at her brother. "You should have seen him yesterday going against Eve and the coyotes. He saved my butt."

Aunt M. curled her fingers at his cheek fuzzed with peach down and gazed at him intently. "What if they rush at you head on?"

"Plaster those losers. A blast in the eyes or snootful of paint will cause a moment's hesitation. Then I'll duck and roll. And I've got my other weapons."

"And Mateo and his gang have assault rifles," she countered, as if anyone needed reminding.

No caution dimmed his shine. "Not if they shift. Can't fire then. I'll be super sneaky around them. Promise, Aunt M."

She lowered her hand, cradling the steaming mug of coffee. Her regretful gaze traced her niece's face and returned to Jimmy's. "Bad enough your sister being a warrior at seventeen. You're only ten."

"Almost eleven," he argued.

"Hardly all grown up. What would your parents say? God rest them."

"That he's quick and clever, and how proud they are. Jimbo excels at everything," Jackson assured their worried relation. "We'll watch out for him."

"Plus he's got a charmed coat. Comes in handy." Morgan anticipated Batboy's response.

He obliged her by wrinkling his nose. "And makes me look like a big bunny. Not that I don't appreciate you making it for me," he hastily added under Miriam's watchful gaze.

"So I should hope." She turned back to the hearth and flipped more pancakes in the iron skillet. The fragrant sizzle mixed with the appetizing aroma of fried bacon and coffee. "Apart from Jimmy's burst of inspiration, what are your plans for our defense, Jackson?"

Eyes shadowed, he pressed fingertips to his temples like a business executive with a high stress job. Those guys had no idea what *real* stress was.

"On short notice?" He gave a whistling sigh. "I'm lining up anyone who will fight with us. Thanks to Morgan, this now includes the Mountain Panteras. I figure Mateo and his gang will strike on the Panther Moon."

"Bound to. Gives us less than a week. But hey, who's counting?" Somberness edged Hawthorne's sarcasm.

"Why then?" Dilly voiced Morgan's unspoken question.

He studied her in bemusement. "The Panteras are stronger during that moon."

She gripped the table. "Than us?"

"Depends on which of *us* you mean." Hawthorne gestured at her. "At least you have the option of popping off if worse comes to worse. Too bad we can't all teleport."

Red hair flew as she shook her head. "I wouldn't abandon my friends. Besides, you're awesome, Hawth. And Morgan's real powerful." She weighed Jackson in a long glance. "You're the strongest of all. Okema left the right one in charge."

Keen insight. At times Dilly was smarter than she let on.

"Sure did," Jimmy chimed in.

Their newly appointed alpha glanced away, reluctance carved in the hollow of his cheek "Perhaps."

Morgan fought the urge to spring across the table, grasp his broad shoulders, and give him a shake. Maybe she'd knock some sense into him. "No *perhaps* about it. You're the seventh Wapicoli, endowed with every bit as much power—more even, Okema said—than I am. The difference between us is you don't want it."

His eyes sparked gold. "You've got that right. And I don't particularly want to lead the Wapicoli into battle either, but I don't have much choice."

Hawthorne raised an imaginary sword. "No. You don't. So mount up, big boy. We're right behind you."

"Or out in front, if you'd rather." Jimmy plowed into a steaming plate of pancakes drizzled with maple syrup and crispy bacon.

Batboy would be. He'd charge ahead of the pack, sword held high. Or fly on Egbert, swooping low to fire arrows.

Lips tight, Jackson shook his head. "Get in line, super kid. I'll lead. It's just, I'd like a word with Okema. Want to know if he's charging in before, during, or after the battle. Because if it's after…"

"You want to be knighted first? Would that make you feel empowered? Sir Jackson, Lord Wolfsbane—" Hawthorne stopped in mid-banter and tilted his head to one side, gray-green eyes contemplative. "Actually, that's not a bad idea."

"Come again?" Jackson frowned at him.

"You need something…" Rubbing his smooth chin, Hawthorne sought for the right word. "*Significant,*" he continued, "to assume your lofty role. Like a knighthood."

"Or a session with *Gandalf,*" Jimmy suggested between bites.

"True. Aragorn would also be inspiring. And Jackson's got a sword." Hawthorne was off and running.

"I'm not sure you can find them." Dilly's brow furrowed in concentration. "I mean, that was a long time ago. Aren't they in heaven by now?"

Her earnest contribution to the exchange had Hawthorne biting back a grin and distracted Jackson from his gloomy focus. He considered her in mock seriousness. "Quite possibly."

Jimmy glanced up. "Kind of heaven. Gandalf, Frodo, and Bilbo sail to the *Undying Lands* with the elves at the end."

"Either way, we'll have to find Jackson someone else." She reached across the table to press his hand. "Don't worry. We will."

Who that would be, Morgan had no idea. A wizard, or profoundly wise shifter...*Glinda*, the good witch of the South...

Maybe the Divining Tree would shed some insight? And maybe the moon was made of green cheese. Getting anything from the age-old oak was more difficult than flying.

Aunt M. skimmed her gaze over the circle. "You four—make that five—beat all. But beneath this zaniness runs a vein of truth. Jackson does need something and someone to anoint him."

"True." Miriam set a plate heaped with pancakes before her grandson. "I know one you might seek out."

Jackson jerked his head around. "Who?"

"The Hermit."

He grimaced. "You mean the old man back in Forgotten Hollow?"

She gave a slight nod.

"Hasn't he got toadstools growing in his beard?"

Jimmy giggled. "And bird poop in his hair like *Radagast*?"

Morgan envisioned the nature loving wizard in *The Hobbit*. "I love the rabbit-sled he drives."

"Awesome." Hawthorne cracked a pretend whip. "That thing's fast. Like a streaking bullet."

"I don't think rabbits would be big enough to pull a sled. Maybe deer? Large ones. With antlers," Dilly suggested.

"Like Santa's sleigh?" Jimmy burst out laughing, inhaled a bite of pancake, and had a coughing fit.

Jackson thumped him on the back and offered him a swig of apple cider. "Easy, Jimbo. I'm betting on a team of buffalo."

Hawthorne beat back a grin. "I'm with Dilly on this one. Definitely eight point bucks," he added, setting Jimmy off again.

"Oh, man." The kid pounded on the table, his eyes streaming with mirth.

"Good grief." Aunt M. buried her head in her hands, but her shoulders shook with muffled laughter.

After Jimmy's paroxysm subsided, Miriam waved at them for their attention. A no-nonsense expression firmed her brown eyes. "I cannot speak to this *Radagast*—not a wizard of my acquaintance—or The Hermit's hygiene. He may well be unkempt. Hermits generally are. But he's wise."

"In an insane sort of way, you mean." Jackson drummed his fingers on the hard oak. "Wonder if he speaks in riddles?"

"If he does, you will figure them out." Miriam remained unencumbered by doubt.

"Great." He raked back his long hair. "Just what I love spending my time trying to decipher."

Actually, Jimmy did. The kid brightened expectantly. "Maybe he talks backward *and* in riddles."

"Double wow," Jackson said gruffly.

"We live in hope." Hawthorne could barely contain himself.

The gifted eccentric had captured Morgan's imagination. "Who is this mystery man?"

Miriam was thoughtful. "Radulf, means 'wolf council' in ancient Germanic."

No point in asking how the woman knew ancient Germanic, she was also versed in Latin. "So he's Wapicoli?"

"On his mama's side. His father was a Mountain Pantera," Miriam added.

"Whoa." Morgan flung up her hands. "I can't imagine either group approved of his parents' marriage."

"Not in the least, so they lived apart. Radulf visits us upon occasion, and sees the Mountain Panteras. Mostly, he keeps to himself." Miriam was matter-of-fact.

"No one has caught sight of him in ages," Hawthorne's soft-spoken mother added. "But we believe he still lives."

"That's good, if you want the kids to visit him." Aunt M.'s eyebrows rose in a question. "What's so unique about The Hermit, apart from his unusual parentage and lack of social skills? Is he a weird blend of Pantera and Wapicoli?"

"He's whatever he likes, a golden panther, a gray wolf, even a big brown bear." Miriam gestured as she spoke, heightening her arms and spreading her hands for each animal. "Mato can best find Radulf for you. He's his great uncle."

Jackson gaped at her. "I never knew."

She grew brisk. "High time you did."

Holy freaking moly. Morgan tried to grasp this odd being. "If he can change form at will, does he have magical powers?"

"Of course." Miriam stirred up the reddish coals in the hearth with an iron poker. Sparks popped and wood smoke scented the cozy kitchen.

The circle of five, plus Aunt Maggie, exchanged widened glances. Jackson came to his senses and straightened. "Okay then. After Rafe and Mato come, we'll seek out Radulf. Anything else we should know about him, Grandma?"

"He's a descendent of the Star People."

"Who isn't?" Snark colored his retort.

Miriam pinned her grandson with a stern eye. "No one else in this kitchen, apart from you and me. Few among the Wapicoli are left to claim that lineage."

"Sorry," he mumbled. "Didn't mean to spurn the honor."

"Then don't." Failing to pay homage to one's elders, no matter who the individual might be, did not sit well with the clan matriarch.

The corners of his mouth crimped and sheepishness hinted in his eyes. "I'll go see Radulf ASAP. Request a knighthood."

"You'll be respectful," she emphasized.

Hand over his heart, he vowed. "Always."

"I'll go, too." Morgan must satisfy her curiosity, and she never knew what might happen on these outings.

"And me." Jimmy wasn't about to be left out. Ever.

"Sign Dilly and me up." Hawthorne fought to subdue the mirth scrunching his face. "Anyone descended from the Star People is a friend of mine."

What did these original space aliens look like, anyway? Were they beautiful celestial beings, or big-eyed creatures with elongated heads and claw-like hands?

Naw. Who the heck would want to mate with them?

Almost involuntarily, she slid her gaze to Jackson and lingered on his dark good looks. Wanting him was a no-brainer.

He met her eyes, his expression a blend of wry humor, exasperation, and leftover awkwardness from upsetting Miriam. "I suppose you've already mastered flying without the wind."

"Sure. One of the ten things I did before breakfast."

"Did not. You slept in." Nothing got past Jimmy. He snapped to attention, seemingly fixated on a spot on the wall. "Hold on." Waggling his fingers the way he did when searching for a word, he blurted. "Got it! Lewis Carroll."

"What is?" The reference was a bit vague even for Batboy.

"'Why, sometimes I've believed as many as six impossible things before breakfast.' Famous quote from the dude who wrote *Alice in Wonderland*." Jimmy was well pleased with himself.

She saluted him. "I'll give you this one."

"Pound it." Jackson bonked fists with the kid.

Aunt M. raised her coffee mug in a toast. "I should get some credit. I taught him to read."

"Credit or blame?" Hawthorne quipped.

"Both, I suppose." She knocked back a swallow.

Bent forward, white knuckling the edge of the table, Dilly circled her gaze at the assembly. "The problem is, those impossible things are *real* here."

Jackson nodded, his manner solemn. "Sure are."

The gravity of their situation wasn't lost on Morgan.

Jimmy remained undeterred, probably couldn't wait to get hold of the super-duper paintball gun. "That's what makes it so cool."

"You say that now—" Jackson began.

"'Then later there's running and um, screaming,'" Hawthorne interjected.

Batboy almost leapt off the bench. "Dr. Ian Malcolm! *The Lost World*!"

"Nailed it." Hawthorne shouldered back with a smile at his partner in geekdom. *Getting* the references was a favorite game.

Even Jackson's lips twitched, and Morgan had to hand it to the kid, evident in her fist pump. But Aunt M., Miriam, and Willow shook their heads, and Dilly regarded the four of them as if they were certifiable.

This, from a witch with a demonic mother and sister. To be fair, though, the girl had only recently realized her unfortunate family circumstances. She'd just become aware of a lot of stuff, and they might all very well be nuts. But they had a battle to win, and some wackiness was necessary to hearten the troops, or in this case—the pack.

Chapter Five
Impossible. Or not.

Miyathwe, the speckled brown owl with a white heart-shaped face, stared at Morgan from the blackened beams overhead. Below, the baby thunderbird dug sharp talons into its wooden block by the hearth. *Give that pterodactyl wannabe plenty of space. Yep*, she was back in the *war room*, as Jimmy and Hawthorne referred to the main room in the great lodge.

The kindred nerds had pinned a large topographical map of the surrounding mountains and Hidden Valley on the log wall to the right of the hearth. An impressive layout of *Middle-earth* commanded a prominent position beside it. Jackson's remark about the necessity for maps hadn't gone unnoted, and he didn't specify which ones he wanted. Heck, maybe orcs were on the clan's growing list of foes.

Their newly appointed alpha, or *sub*, as Jackson preferred to think of himself, like a coach stepping in until the *real one* returned, stood before the more pertinent visual. His tall figure cast a long shadow in the flickering flames.

"Cool. Shows every rise and dip of the land." He slid his index finger over the ridges and tapped a sunken spot. "Here it is. *Lost Hollow*. Our next destination."

Morgan parked beside him, inhaling his masculine

essence. "Where your knighthood awaits."

"Or whatever," he muttered, something he did a lot of lately.

"That, too." Hoping he'd spare her a glance, she'd slicked her lips with gloss, dabbed on the scent Miriam made from bramble roses and deep woods' spice berries, and pulled her hair up in a high ponytail. Pale gold curls tumbled over her shoulders, catching the light when she swished her hair.

The black leather pants and jacket were her usual warrior attire. Beneath it, she wore a white blouse with a lace-up bodice. The height of feminine. What more could a Morcant girl do? Hiking boots were a necessity, and heels out of the question. This was as good as she got. If Jackson didn't find her appealing enough to take notice, she was at a loss.

He glanced around, though not at her. The orange glow from the fire played over his perfect profile. "Breaking news, guys. They're here."

"Right." She detected the light footfall.

"Who?" Dilly wore her usual puzzled expression. They really should all chip in and buy the poor girl a clue.

Hawthorne circled an arm around her shoulders where they sat together on the couch. "Mato and Rafe."

No need to tip Jimmy off. The kid was bounding toward the door. He'd make an excellent watch dog.

Faded green rucksacks slung on their backs, the two young men strode into the room. Each lifted their right hand in greeting. "All hail," they intoned in low voices.

"All hail," the gathering echoed.

Jimmy pawed them like a puppy, his eyes on the

paintball rifle hanging over Rafe's shoulder. He grinned and slipped the prize into Jimmy's eager grasp. "I believe you ordered this."

"Epic!" Batboy jigged the dance of joy.

Lips curving, Jackson nodded at the new arrivals. "*Megwich*. What about Ray and Joe?"

Jackson's Uncle Ray and his sidekick, Dilly's warlock father, Joe, would complete the fellowship on their arrival.

Rafe removed his camo cap and ran a hand through lengths of chestnut-brown hair. "Dad and Joe are getting things straight so Mom can mind the store while they're away, and rescheduling a gig for the band. They'll be here in a day or two."

"Hope Armageddon holds off that long." Jackson didn't appear entirely certain. Neither was Morgan.

Whistling through his teeth, Rafe gave a half-nod, half-shrug. "We probably have until the Panther Moon to ready ourselves. Four to five days—depending."

Some allotted a greater time span to the full moon cycle and counted three days total, instead of only one. The moon effect varied between werewolves. There were those who succumbed earlier to its pull, and others who resisted.

Mato slid his pack to the floor. "What's our quest this time? Defeat Mateo and save the Wapicoli? Anything else?"

"One or two other possible nemesis to battle. No biggie." Hawth sprang to his feet and clapped Mato on his beefy shoulder. They did the bands' *slap, slap, chop, chop, pound it* handshake. "We're at Defcon One."

"That good, huh? About as usual then." Mato

waved to Dilly. "How are you holding up with this crew, girl?"

Blue-green eyes outlined in mauve liner shone. "Fine. Except they should all be wearing tinfoil hats."

The big bearwalker grinned. "What else is new?"

"No telling. We're sure glad y'all came." Dilly leapt up. Flinging out her arms, she gestured the group close. "Come on, everybody. Group hug."

No one else, except maybe Jimmy, would've attempted this with a bunch of guys. But the teen witch, who scarcely knew she was one, urged the assembly together. They each encircled the person or persons nearest them—Mato engulfed three—until they were all connected. Morgan had to admit the affirmation of their close-knit bond was heartening.

Lord only knew what lay ahead of them. Vital that they had each other. The scents she breathed in signified family, friendship, and passion for Jackson. Above all, these unique beings were her pack. There wasn't a soul here she wouldn't give her life for if she must.

Power emanated from the circle. Energy filled the wood smoke-tinged air and auras swirled around her in shades of blue, violet, and yellow. Jackson's simmered orange-gold, a meld of brooding and the inner fire he inherently possessed. By birthright, his aura should be bluish-white with a silver sheen, like Okema's. Overriding moodiness had him dipping into the broader color palette.

Red joined the vibrant spectrum with the adventurous Rafe and Mato. The latter shared in the silvery shimmer of wisdom cloaking Miriam. A swathe of psychic purple also encircled the wise healer when she was near, but she and Willow were in the kitchen preparing a celebratory supper. Only the core of Jackson's pack had gathered in here.

Heads bowed, they huddled close. "'May the force be with us,'" Hawthorne inserted in the near sacred silence, from his spot between Dilly and Rafe.

Typical Hawth. Morgan figured he couldn't resist.

"May it, indeed." Jackson broke the circle and stepped back. Others followed his lead.

A rainbow of colors lit Jimmy, clasping the army styled rifle that fired glow-in-the-dark paint pellets. He'd barely had an arm free for the hug of solidarity, but was in the crush by Mato.

"Thought you might need this." Rafe knelt and unzipped a pocket on his pack. "Brought plenty of ammo."

"Awesome." Batboy was in heaven.

Rafe handed over a camo pouch with a strap. "Wanna go outside and practice?"

No need to ask Jimmy twice. He bolted from the room. "Get your coat and stay near the lodge!" Morgan shouted after him.

Jackson eyed her in faint amusement. "Don't fret, *mommy*. He knows the drill."

Her cheeks warmed. "Suppose I do sound mommified."

"You think? What are you gonna do when he's out riding that?" He pointed at Egbert perched on his block at the corner of the fireplace, the spot everyone took care to avoid. Only Jimmy could safely handle the bird who'd attached itself to him upon hatching. The others risked a hissing peck.

"I swear it's grown overnight." The infant dragon

fluttered more vigorously against the tether, its open beak seeking handouts. "I have no clue what to do when Batboy mounts up," she admitted.

"In a week or two at this rate." Jackson tossed the ever hungry raptor a mouse pellet from the sack Jimmy had stowed nearby. "And I think it's a *he*, which means this bird's gonna get really big."

Rafe chuckled. "I can seriously see super kid flying him."

"Me too." A vivid picture soared through Morgan's mind. "Aunt M. may have a few qualms."

"I'll bet." Mato surveyed Egbert from his stance before the hearth, his large figure basked in flames, glossy brown mane falling around his wide shoulders. "I'm wagering on wonder boy winning the day."

When it came right down to it, so was Morgan. "Jimmy finds a way."

Mato was in his contemplative mode. He might've been a lumberjack in the heavy plaid shirt and jeans, but she knew better. He was a bear whenever he liked, and not when he didn't, and wise whichever he was.

"Good thing the kid's on our side. Little brother told us about your flying thing. You've upped the blue light special. Impressive." He high-fived her with his much larger hand.

Respect in his appreciative gaze, Rafe clapped palms with her. "Way to go. We'll need every power shot we can get."

Their praise was uplifting. "*Megwich*. I'm learning."

"You'll get there. Amaze us all." Rafe sounded absolutely confident, and Mato nodded his affirmation.

"Wow. Thanks for the vote of confidence."

Why neither of these two had a girlfriend mystified her. If she weren't magnetically drawn to Jackson, she'd certainly consider the eighteen-year-old Rafe with his Wapicoli good looks. Mato was well into his twenties, a fab catch for some woman. Maybe he didn't want to be caught?

Such romantic conjectures likely never crossed Jackson's mind. Having the weight of leadership thrust upon him had snared his full attention. She hoped he'd be buoyed by the reunion of the fellowship, and would find a place in his weighty cares for her. She might be a sack of potatoes for all the notice he'd given her, and she was no sack.

Mato gestured at her and Jackson. "Are you two running this operation together?"

She cast their commando leader a reproachful look. "We're not *co-doing* anything lately."

The newcomers exchanged glances.

"Here we go," Hawthorne said under his breath.

"And she's wearing gloss and done her hair," Dilly added, as if the effects should rock Jackson's world.

He turned eyes brimming with intensity on Morgan, and waved the others aside. "Allow us a moment, guys and gal." Bending his head, he pressed his lips to her ear. "What's going on here?" he hissed. "I'm trying to plan battle strategy. Sure, I'd rather be cozying up with you. Night and day. Not an option."

"Could have fooled me," she whispered back, secretly pleased by his annoyance and assertion.

"I didn't realize Okema was gonna split and I'd have to take over. Requires a little scheming."

She circled her arms around his neck. "I could help, you know. I'm not exactly stupid."

"But definitely distracting."

A thrill rippled through her. "About time you noticed."

"Oh no." He closed an arm around her waist, triggering more shivers. "The distraction is not new."

"Good. If an apocalypse is at hand, I don't want to go down unappreciated."

He glowered at her, desire in the depths of his fiery gaze. "Zero chance of that."

She smiled slightly. "So you love the hair?"

He snorted. "Yeah. And the gloss is to die for." Humor touched his eyes and he tilted her back. "I should drop you smack on the floor, since you can fly—"

Mato cleared his throat. "Sorry to interrupt your tender moment, fight, or whatever this is. Just wondered if you've had any trouble with vampires?"

"What?" Jackson snatched Morgan close and did an about-face, taking her with him. He clutched her in a near death hold, and she held to him.

Every eye honed in on the bearwalker. He gave a noncommittal shrug. "Probably just talk."

"By whom?" Their sub-chief went rigid.

"Walkers. Mostly."

"So, the bears." Judging by Jackson's expression, his mind was in hyperdrive. He rounded on his newly arrived cousin. "What have you heard?"

Rafe spread both hands. "Might be nothing."

"There's a heck of a difference between absolutely not and maybe." Jackson wasn't amused.

Not a hint of humor danced in Hawthorne's eyes. Normally, he was irrepressible. Unnerving to witness him so taken aback. And Dilly had gone white. Morgan suspected she'd paled too. Blood suckers weren't on her party list.

Jackson held up his hand. "Let me get this straight. In addition to Okema disappearing without a word, Mateo and his Panteras breathing down our necks, Dilly's coyote witch sister and her pack, whom we've underestimated, by the way, circling like sharks, her lizard mother lying awake nights plotting our demise, and Morgan's crazed Uncle Don and his renegade wolves after our territory—" He ticked the names off his fingers. "Now you've heard *talk* of vampires? They don't freakin' exist!"

"That's what we thought." Doubt shadowed Mato's brown gaze, and Rafe glanced away from Jackson's volatile stare.

He dropped his simmering disbelief to Morgan. "Better power up, Wolf Girl, and pray the Hermit knows his stuff. I'm gonna need that knighthood."

She had the distinct impression she would, too. And soon. "What kills them?"

"You mean the non-existent vamps?" Jackson tossed his hair back like a rocker and thrummed his fingers on the mantel. "We'll have to ask Grandma Miriam what she'd suggest."

"I'm here." The cloaked figure spoke from across the room. Her batlike sonar must've honed in on their distress signal and drawn her to them. "Vampires can't tolerate belladonna, wolfsbane, or mountain ash in any quantity."

Jackson flashed gold eyes at her. "Neither can we."

Two were poisonous herbs and the third a sacred tree used to repel dark forces. For some reason, werewolves qualified, no matter how good Morgan tried to be. Go figure.

Miriam brushed aside his concern. "I'll brew a potent potion. Tip your arrows in it, and don't shoot anything or anyone you don't intend to kill." Her silver hair shone and beaded earrings glinted as she neared the subdued gathering by the hearth. "Vampires incinerate in bright sunlight, and don't hold up well to having their heads separated from their bodies. A stake through the heart is also effective."

"So, swords, stakes, bows and arrows," Jackson mused aloud, meeting his grandmother's gaze. "What about bullets?"

"No effect. The Panteras will have a rude awakening. Although, their razor sharp teeth and claws are an advantage. And their speed. You're fast too. Only the oldest vampires can teleport."

Jackson eyed her in wonder. "How long have you known about them?"

"Always. No need to cause alarm when none have been spotted in these ridges for over two centuries. Okema and I agreed not to mention them."

Morgan gaped at her. "Why now?"

"Because he's gone, and we're more vulnerable. This is why you have come to us." She swept her hand at the gathering. "Why you've all been called together." She directed a finger ringed with silver bands at her grandson. "Why you must seek out Radulf and claim your destiny."

Again, her prophetic eyes rested on Morgan. "You, too, have far more power than you yet know. Our hope lies with you and Jackson. With you all."

Part of Morgan wanted to ask Miriam more, and part of her hesitated. "What of Okema? Will he return?"

"In his time. No creature is stronger than Okema. Until then, we must do battle."

"With vampires?" Hawthorne gave an exaggerated shudder. "Man. 'Just when you think it's safe to go back into the water.'" At least, he hadn't permanently abandoned all humor.

Jackson shook his head. "It's never safe."

Didn't Morgan know? "Are they ever good? Vampires, I mean."

Dilly eyed her as if she'd missed the obvious. "This isn't *Twilight,* girlfriend."

Crap. Even the ditz knew.

Miriam raised a cautioning hand. "Some vampires have the ability to mesmerize. Resist at all costs. You are their equals and their betters. Remember that."

With a prickling chill, Morgan resolved to stab her new foe, or foes, through the heart should any cross her path—or rip their heads off. It made little difference to her, as long as the Wapicoli prevailed. And she'd resisted Lilith's hypnotic gorgon-like gaze. How much worse could a vamp's be?

She didn't care to discover.

Okema, please come back.

Buffy the Vampire Slayer was also welcome.

In lieu of either one, Morgan supposed she and Jackson would have to go and get their knighthoods. By jingo, by heaven, by golly, or however the saying went, that Radulf dude wasn't leaving her out. She also needed more *uummpphh* for this increasingly impossible quest.

Chapter Six
Is It Just Me?

Typical brisk afternoon in the mountains, right? Morgan wasn't so sure.

True, the autumn woods *appeared* the same. The windblown forest scent mingled with her six companions and the animals who lived here in a familiar aromatic meld. Underfoot, a fragrant whiff of wintergreen rose from the green mats dotted with red partridge berries vining over the leaf strewn trail. Overhead, bare branches and evergreen boughs tossed against a sky banked with clouds. Nut-crazed squirrels scurried up and down furrowed trunks. Chipmunks darted over a toppled giant oak covered with moss and buttery yellow lichens. The gurgle of a stream flowed nearby.

Everything seemed normal, except for the murmurings that didn't belong. What was with that?

Panteras didn't murmur. Neither did Eve and her coyotes, or Uncle Don and his wolves. They'd spring soundlessly without warning from the hazy underbrush, unless their tight band detected them first. Who did this leave, and why couldn't she discern their presence?

No one else in the pack seemed bothered. All the shifters had a keen sense of smell and hearing. Precious little escaped their hawk eyes. Nothing got past Jackson, and Jimmy was practically a super kid. If she missed something—highly unlikely—they'd pick up on any trespassers. Surely she wasn't imagining it?

Glancing from side-to-side, she combed the misty woods, and closed gloved fingers around the bow strap at her chest. She might need to fly into action any second. "Is it just me, or does anyone else hear whispering voices?"

"Only the wind." Jimmy followed at her heels, glorying in the paintball rifle he'd added to his weapon arsenal.

"It's never just the wind," Jackson flung over his shoulder, his breath showing white in the cold air. He headed their line directly in front of her, strands of long hair whipping beneath his dark brown fedora. The narrow trail kept them single file.

"I don't know about voices, but we're in for sleet or snow. Remind me again why we aren't speeding along on dirt bikes?" Hawthorne's snide tone carried from behind Jimmy. Rafe, and Mato brought up the rear of their party.

Jackson grunted his disapproval. "For sneaking through the woods? Ranks next to chainsaws for a muffled approach."

"At least we'd get there faster." Hawth had gotten it into his head that their new alpha could/should change Okema's ban on anything noise making.

Dirt bikes topped the chief's list of no no's. This didn't mean the guys hadn't collected a few, plus several four wheelers, secluded back at the lodge. But these were for goofing around, not a deadly serious mission.

"Bringing the pickups was a stretch when we're on red alert," Jackson reminded his querulous cousin.

"They're not exactly super silent, and we had to abandon them."

They'd left the trucks along the rutted edge of what passed for a road, more of a washed out creek bed, before it further deteriorated into a footpath.

"Faster my way, and we'd still be on the bikes." Hawth was in his dog/wolf with a bone mood.

Jackson flung up gloved fingers. "Or battling for our lives. With—take your pick of foes. Maybe all of them."

"Well, excuse me for thinking we're in a hurry to reach Radulf and get back, what with the Panther Moon coming up—"

"And all," Jimmy finished for his fellow nerd.

Hawthorne's tread was more like kick the ground than a stealthy walk. "No rush. Nothing important we've got to do," he groused. "Just save the world."

"Well, *our* world, anyway," Rafe amended. "Not sure how far-reaching these evils are if we don't stop them."

"Dude, are you hearing yourself?" If he'd expressed doubts about *Middle-earth*, Hawthorne couldn't sound more incredulous. "Have you forgotten the whole shadow spreading thing? You know what unhindered evil does."

"Grows bigger. Engulfs all mankind, and shifters," Rafe intoned dutifully.

"The whole world." Morgan felt it to her core.

"Guys," Jimmy interrupted. "Are those clouds, or smoke?" He pointed upward. "Over there."

The wispy tendrils rising above the trees barely stood out in the haze. She inhaled the frosty forest scent tinged with the hint of hickory. "I smell a wood fire."

"Yeah," they all agreed in unison.

"Must be a hearth around here somewhere." She glanced back at Mato, muted by the mist. "Could it be your uncle's?"

"Highly probable. I haven't seen Uncle Radulf in years. The last time I visited, though, he lived in a cave in this neck of the woods."

Great. "Must be the Pantera in him, if he takes after that side of the family."

Mato shifted his bulky pack. He carried the most supplies in case they were delayed. "Don't jump to conclusions. He also has a small cabin hangout. A tiny version of Wapicoli Lodge."

The added info doubled her wonder. "So he takes after *both* sides?"

Mato nodded. "Plus he's a bearwalker."

"Does he know if he's coming or going?" Hawthorne probably spoke for them all.

"A bit moody, as I recall, but he's the wisest man I've ever met, next to Okema." Not a trace of doubt edged Mato's assurance, and Miriam had vouched for his eccentric relation.

"They hardly qualify as 'men' in the traditional sense." Hawthorne's argumentative streak bore on, probably spurred by suspicion regarding Radulf, boredom with the bikeless hike, and frustration that Jackson wasn't sympathetic to his wishes.

Okema chose wisely when he left his grandson in charge, plus there was the whole seventh Wapicoli thing with him.

"How much farther?" Jimmy was definitely bored.

She sniffed. "The smoke's stronger. We must be getting closer."

The strange sounds also increased. They resembled faint voices, but not in any language she understood. More like a garbled mix. "Seriously, guys. No one else hears odd whispers?"

"No. And you really should stop listening," Hawthorne advised. "You'll need one of those tinfoil hats next thing."

"Or listen harder and figure it out." Rafe's take made more sense.

"Maybe you're getting signals from the Mother Ship." A typical Jimmy response.

"Or not," Hawthorne countered. "Could be something insidious. Do they sound evil or heavenly?"

"Neither. Exactly." She couldn't describe it.

Jackson paused and turned toward her, his brow creased beneath the brim of his hat. "Why are you the only one hearing this?"

The concern in his expression sent a chill crawling down her back, and not from the nippy woods. "No clue. Wish I knew."

He gestured at her. "What about that magical moonstone of yours?"

She instinctively patted her necklace. "It's never ceased emitting a barely detectable hum, but nothing like this."

He weighed her in a long glance. "Could it have upped the signal and your special bond tapped you into the broadcast?"

"Maybe, but—" She waved her hand at the tossing branches and gray clouds. "This seems to be coming from everywhere."

Hawthorne gave an impatient snort. "We're back to the wind again."

Jackson shook his head. "Morgan can tell the difference. This could be anything or anyone."

"Yeah," she agreed uneasily, while appreciating his belief in her.

"Let's hope Radulf has some answers." He pivoted and resumed the hike. "And we're not in for a lot of *riddle me this* crap."

Jimmy loved that stuff, but she got his point. Time was of the essence. "Mato," she summoned, as quietly as she could while making himself heard over the bluster. You never knew who might be listening. "What's your uncle like?"

"Kind of like me, only older. So good looking. Or was."

"Right." His reply left a lot of wiggle room.

"Ray and Joe might know more. But by the time they arrive, we will have already been, and returned to the lodge. Fingers or paws crossed," he added.

Jackson grasped his sword hilt, as ready for the not-so-legendary vampires as possible, until the poisonous arrows were prepared for firing. "My dad only said Radulf was worth a visit. With all the work he and Uncle Buck have to do while we're off, he couldn't stop for a chat."

Not that Peter Wapicoli was much of a talker, anyway. She'd seen him and Buck chopping firewood before they left, and there was always hunting to do, and readying for the impending battle. They had knives to sharpen, another sword to forge (hers), arrows needed dipping in Miriam's lethal brew, and someone had to toss mouse nuggets to the voracious thunderbird. Aunt M. and Dilly helped where they could, as did other Wapicoli.

"I hear you," Mato grunted. "Few know Radulf well enough to say. He mostly keeps to himself. He's one of a kind."

This summed up everything she'd heard about the mystery man. Now, to meet this bearwalker/Pantera/Wapicoli known as The Hermit and pray he'd be of help.

In the strange garble of noises around her, she detected, *Divining Tree.* Maybe this was worth a mention?

She couldn't imagine vamps talked gibberish on some celestial loudspeaker, and they should know nothing of the tree. The ancient oak was a guarded secret. Wasn't it?

Chapter Seven
Radulf's Hangout

Finally. Journey's end was in sight and Morgan eager for warmth and shelter. Lacy snowflakes fell against the log cabin tucked among the shrouded trees ahead of them. The sugary coating frosted the gingerbread-like house. Relief washed over her. The trailing smoke came from the stone chimney, not a smutty cave.

"Oh, good. We don't have to go underground." Not appealing to her, especially in this weather.

"Looks like Radulf's got a sweet crib." Hawthorne's humor was somewhat restored. Nothing kept him down for long.

"I've never heard that said of my humble abode. However, I must confess few folk have visited me over the years," a low voice remarked from the trees to their right.

Morgan's heart lodged in her throat. Everyone swiveled toward the cloaked figure emerging from the cluster of evergreens, his tread as hushed as the falling snow. The blue effervescent sheen encircling him must account for no one detecting his scent.

She gaped at him in amazement. He could've stepped out of a fairytale. A wide-brimmed black felt hat, dusted white, covered his head, and silver hair cascaded over a cloak made of fur pelts that appeared

Medieval. Maybe it was.

The beard reaching mid-chest matched his hair. She couldn't be certain of his features in the filmy curtain of flakes, but he had a long nose, pursed lips, and silvery eyes. No wait. They were gold. No reddish. Silver again.

What the heck? His eyes changed like the thoughts whirring through Dilly's mind.

Radulf's variable gaze circled their group, frozen to the powdery trail. Even Mato seemed taken aback. Their apparent host acknowledged them with outstretched hands. "Pardon my abrupt entry. I get so little company, I forget myself." With a sweep of his long fingers, he gestured them ahead. "Please join me. It grows late. As you are Wapicoli, and travel with my nephew, I assumed you would be more comfortable in the cabin than the cave. I am perfectly amenable to both."

While the others stood in shocked silence, their sub-chief stepped forward. Radulf was so tall, even Jackson tilted his head to meet his gaze. "*Megwich*, Radulf. We thank you for receiving our party. Grandmother Miriam speaks highly of you."

"And I of her. A worthy woman." He beckoned to them and proceeded ahead. High-top moccasins left footprints in the fresh cover. Undeniable proof of his reality.

"Your need is great. These are dark times, my friends." He flipped his fingers over his shoulder as if tossing something behind them. A glimmer shone in the whiteness. "A concealing spell is called for, I think. You do realize you're being followed?"

"No," Jackson confessed, speaking for them all.

"Any pursuers are not close enough for us to scent. Though I anticipate trouble returning to the lodge."

"That you shall have."

Radulf's solemn assurance sent more chills prickling down Morgan's spine. Not that she was surprised, but *come on*, couldn't they at least make it back to the lodge and regroup first? Hopes they had until the Panther Moon dimmed.

Mato's ground-covering stride soon had him beside his mysterious relation. "Who do you detect, uncle?"

"An old evil, a new evil, and a threat with whom I believe you may yet reconcile."

Jackson swiveled his head at the obscured forest then returned his focus to Radulf. "Do you mean to say we are pursued by every foe?"

"Not all maintain the same position in the woodland, but yes. They are on your trail."

Stopping in his tracks, Jackson raised both hands. "What are we to do? Fight them all? We're not yet ready."

Even in his alarm, he had more self-control than Morgan who blurted, "Holy freakin' crap."

The wizard, for this is what he was in addition to a highly versatile shifter, halted and turned toward her. "You know where to go and from whom to seek help."

His silvery—no blue—eyes pierced hers, and a voice in her head said, 'The Divining Tree. The Star People.'

He gave her a moment to process the message, then nodded. "You heard rightly. Yet there is more than this you must learn. I commend you on forming an alliance with Santiago, Wolf Girl. You shall need it." He motioned their stunned band forward. "Come, refresh yourselves. We will speak further."

Hardly able to believe Radulf or the non-verbal message she'd received, she fell in behind Jackson and Mato who walked on either side of the man/wizard/multi-shifter. The others followed in unusual stillness. He'd even stumped Batboy, and Hawth was rarely ever this quiet. Rafe had gone mute.

"Enter, friends." Radulf opened the cabin door and waited as they walked inside, then ducked beneath the lintel and slid the sturdy bolt into place. With the stout barrier secured, the blowing snow instantly ceased.

"No one enters without my leave." He cast a glimmer of sparks at the door, much as he'd flung them over his shoulder earlier in the woods.

A protective spell, maybe, in case anybody got past his last one. The dude was definitely reassuring to have around. With her fears lessened, her natural inclinations turned to thoughts of food.

Mmmmm. The meaty scent of stew mixed with pungent herbs and wood smoke. And what a snug cabin. After hours out in the raw cold, she was grateful for this welcome refuge. No doubt, her astonished companions were, too. Like them, she ran her gaze over Radulf's cozy house.

The interior wasn't as small as she'd expected after viewing it from the outside, and he had far more seating than she anticipated. Visions of sitting cross-legged on the floor before the hearth vanished at the sight of hand-hewn chairs fashioned of vines and bent twigs, Wapicoli style. Two were placed on either side of the oak table, and a fancier, high-backed chair stood at each end. He also had stools for any spillover. Either he was a skilled craftsman who enjoyed woodworking, or knew a guy who was.

Woven baskets filled with dried herbs and ropes of braided onions hung from the blackened beams overhead. An owl similar to Miyathwe peered down at her from his perch on the rafters. The bird was a wizardly sort of companion. A crow or raven would also work. She almost expected to see one.

She spied the loft above them. A wooden ladder provided access for those who couldn't scale the distance in a single bound. The murky hideaway was laden with piles of fur, blankets, and trunks, a hodgepodge of stuff. Even wizards needed an attic, she supposed, turning her inspection to the shelves built along one log wall crammed with antiquated books and curios. Intricately carved boxes containing heaven only knew what were lodged beside stones and crystals of various shapes and colors.

Magic rocks, maybe? What about the assortment of feathers? Were they magic, too, or used in spells? Either that, or he sure liked feathers.

A rattle of pots sounded through the doorway leading off the back of this main room. The tread of slippered feet was followed by an older woman who bustled toward them wiping her hands on a linen towel. She had a Mountain Pantera scent about her. Wisps of gray hair escaped the purple scarf knotted around her head. A thick braid bound with ribbons fell down her back. The flamboyant blouse and flowered skirts showing beneath her shockingly pink apron weren't at all what Morgan expected. Neither were the pink-flowered slippers. But then, she hadn't expected anyone in this cabin except Radulf. Didn't hermits, by definition, live alone?

He gestured at the color-mad woman. "This is Birdie. You can already tell she's from Santiago's clan. He thought I needed a bit of help in my advancing years, and sent her to cook and clean for me."

"And a sight more than that," Birdie mumbled, but a smile creased her lined face and revealed strong white teeth.

Admittedly, it was good of Santiago to remember his half-Pantera relation. Had the Wapicoli helped with Radulf's distinctive furnishings?

Birdie's green eyes shone. Fortunately, she held no apparent grudge against the newcomers. "Welcome. We've been expecting you."

With a wizard in the house, Morgan didn't ask how. For all she knew, Birdie might also be psychic.

"The cornbread's ready and I'm dishing up the stew," their hostess continued. "Make yourselves at home. If anyone needs the bathroom, it's through there." She waved a wrinkled hand at another door.

"Birdie insisted we put that in, and the kitchen," Radulf explained, while Morgan tried to imagine him doing anything as mundane as plumbing. Maybe the Panteras had assisted. They must have small kitchens and bathrooms in their caravans.

"The water comes from the stream and uses gravity for natural flow," he added.

"Cool." Jimmy approved the engineering behind this feat.

Running water must account for the taps and porcelain sink she glimpsed in the room behind the gypsy housekeeper. A black lead cook stove dominated another corner. It probably dated from the eighteen hundreds and the sink was old-fashioned, but the cabin had amenities that made life easier.

Smiling proudly, Birdie flicked her towel at their surroundings. "Got the place fixed up real nice, don't you think?"

"Really nice," Morgan agreed, with a grunt of assents from her companions.

Birdie put her slippered foot down. "When Radulf's in his cave, I stay here."

"Yeah." Morgan would, too.

In fact, given the enemies on their tail ranging from the 'Big Bad' Mateo and his city gang, the ever-scheming Lilith, witchy Eve and her coyotes, crazed Uncle Don and his renegade werewolves, and vampires with yet unplumbed powers, she was tempted to stay here permanently. But she couldn't, not with the world to save.

How hard would those concealing/protection spells be to learn, or did she have to be born with the power? What else might she glean from Radulf? She couldn't begin to fathom what lay behind those ever-changing eyes. Fortunately, for them, he was a much-needed ally.

A large black bird flew down from the dusky rafters and landed on his fur covered shoulder. "Eat up," he croaked, in a hoarse voice.

She knew it! *A crow*. Hadn't expected a talking one, though. This made two feathered companions and a housekeeper named Birdie residing under Radulf's roof. He must be partial to winged creatures. She hoped he possessed equal fondness for werewolves. He was part Wapicoli, along with everything else.

She and Jackson—all of them—needed as much help as he could give. Time was fast running out, their enemies nearing, and the Panther Moon would lend the

Panteras, including Mateo and his gang, extra strength. She had no idea what it did for vampires. Or Star People. Maybe it didn't matter to space aliens, but it sure as heck did to everyone else.

Chapter Eight
Wizard's Blessing

Birdie's cooking was so tasty Morgan thought it might be charmed like Lilith's moonshine, but the goodhearted gypsy was the opposite of the Mountain Witch. Ravenous hunger brought on by hours out in the bone-numbing cold probably had some bearing on her rapt appreciation of the food. Whatever the reason, she refrained from snapping up the savory stew like a dog, um, wolf.

A surround sound of muffled slurps, the scrape of spoons on empty bowls, readily refilled by the eager cook, and avid munching compensated for the lack of dinner conversation. Why talk, when you could eat? And they did. The way they tore into the rich broth heaped with meat and vegetables, you'd think this was their last supper.

Shoot fire and spit tomatoes, as Uncle Don used to say, maybe it was. A pang ran through her at the memory of her once jovial relation and his collection of countryisms. He'd been fun, and now, a power-crazed mad wolf had taken his place. Jackson had warned Morcant males often make bad werewolves. Siblings shouldn't bite siblings, an act Aunt M. deeply regretted, and one Morgan was determined not to commit.

Swiping at the tear she hoped no one noticed, she returned her focus to the meal and their host. He'd removed his hat and ancient-looking mantle before supper and hung them behind the door on a wooden peg. The group's snowy outer wear were suspended from spots on other pegs along the log wall.

Beneath his cloak, Radulf wore what she'd swear was a colonial styled white shirt. Birdie, the mistress of color, must've created his quilted vest made of vibrant patches. High, fur-lined moccasins met his brown wool pants below the knees; no fancy sewing there, but craftsmanship.

His changeable eyes met Morgan's searching gaze, and she sensed how much he knew about her. *About everything.*

The tips of his fingers pressed against his temples, he surveyed the gathering. He had far less zeal for the scrumptious bounty spread before him than they did. Maybe he'd eaten a big lunch—yesterday. She'd never figured out when Okema ate, apart from the few times he'd joined them at the lodge.

Fortunately, provisions were plentiful or the hand reaching for the last square of cornbread might've been stabbed with a fork. Birdie saved them from a food fight by padding out with another platter of steaming yellow cakes slathered in honey. Hot coffee was also plentiful. Even Jimmy had a mugful with sugar and lots of milk from Birdie's nanny goat in the lean-to. There were no cows in this remote place, or a grocery store for convoluted miles. Supplies had to last a while, and Morgan hoped they hadn't depleted their stock.

The scent of cinnamon on the air, the cook triumphantly bore out fragrant apple dumplings. Cheers and clapping greeted her hot-from-the-oven desert.

Mato gave a whistle. "Way to go, Birdie!"

"Aww, get on with you." She waved a shooing gesture, beaming at their praise. Guests at her table were a rare occurrence for one who took pride in her culinary achievements, and clearly, she did. Cooking for an eccentric wizard must have its drawbacks.

Contented sighs rippling around her, Morgan sagged in her seat. She'd love to curl up by the hearth on the bearskin rug and sleep. Probably, they all would.

Radulf cleared his throat. "Time is short."

Why was it never *long*?

He rose to his feet and snapped his fingers. "Hither thee dee."

Who the—what the—? She swiveled her head. Were they expecting someone through the barred, enchanted door?

At Radulf's unusual—Okay, weird—summons, the crow flew from his dusky haunt among the rafters and landed on the wizard's shoulder. Eyes bright, he remained in place as Radulf strode to the hearth and turned to face his wondering guests.

Was *Hither Thee Dee* the bird's name or a call signal? Fortunately, Jimmy and Hawthorne were too impressed even for a whispered quip, which she suspected their sharp-eared, likely psychic, host would detect.

The blue effervescent sheen outlining him shone in the firelight, as did his silver hair and flowing beard. He might've have been Merlin, garbed rather differently than she imagined that legendary wizard would've been. The effect on her was the same as if she'd beheld Merlin, awe, and more than a little intimidation. He and Okema would make quite a pair.

He waved them near. "Bring your seats and settle

in. Morgan and Jackson, center front."

Of course. Their place now. Steeling herself, she rose.

Everyone except Birdie, scurrying to and from the kitchen, drew their chairs close to the comforting crackle. She and Jackson sat side-by-side while the others positioned themselves in a semi-circle around them; Mato and Rafe to their right, Hawthorne and Jimmy to their left.

She slid her gaze to Jackson, sitting with his head up, jaw firm, and slipped her hand into his welcoming grasp. He gave her fingers a reassuring squeeze before she balled them in her lap. Who could promise them anything? Radulf's gaze hinted at sternness. That didn't bode well.

Tense, expectant, she waited for him to speak. They all did. Kindling popped and showery sparks hissed in the grate while they sat in suspense.

He considered them for a piercing moment. "Too long have you warred with the Panteras, and they with you. I stand here, the embodiment of both, and in alignment with the bears."

They watched, slack-jawed, as he shifted into a dazzling golden-orange panther, then a silvery gray wolf, and a great brown bear with pools of wisdom in its dark eyes. All the while, the crow perched on whatever sufficed as his shoulder, adjusting to his changes in one fluid motion.

No one stirred. Morgan hardly dared to breathe, let alone inquire which animal shape was his favorite. She hoped the wolf.

He assumed his human form again, and opened his mouth. "Remember your new allegiance to Santiago.

He will honor his side of the accord Morgan struck with the mountain leader. Mateo has ever been driven by vengeance and greed, and with him, his kind. But not all. Never all. Even now, hope remains."

His gaze rested on her. "Your uncle is not entirely lost to you. He may yet be persuaded to an alliance."

She met his soul-searching scrutiny. "But Uncle Don is possessed with the madness that comes to Morcant men. I wish with all my heart he had resisted this insanity, but I've witnessed what he's become." She winced at the sharp memory.

Empathy softened Radulf's gold—no blue—eyes. "I, too, have seen what he is. Also what he was." He lightly tapped one finger on her forehead. "In here. I ask you to consider that the man you knew may still exist beneath the craze, at least, in part. If you present sound argument to him, he may yet side with the Wapicoli. How are he and his band to withstand the growing forces against them with no ally?"

How indeed? Torn between love for Uncle Don and gut-knotting apprehension of what he'd become, she pondered Radulf's words. Her intent companions likely did the same.

Grandma Sarah's advice, written two centuries ago for her, returned in her tumbled thoughts. *Listen to the deepest recesses of your innermost self. Heed the wisdom it imparts, and that of those who have earned your trust.*

Maybe, just maybe, there might be a way. She slowly nodded. "If the opportunity arises, I will do as you ask and attempt to reason with him."

Jackson sidled his boots. "You know what he did to your aunt. He's violent in the extreme. How can you trust him to get near enough to speak?"

"Morgan is more powerful than Uncle Don," Jimmy said simply. "And I'll help her."

Tender pride warmed her at his affirmation and support, especially after their uncle's cruel rejection of him. Batboy was also far stronger than their lost relation realized.

Jackson weighed her with a pensive air. "Another Wapicoli Morcant alliance would bolster our side. And where the alpha goes, his pack will follow. But it'll be like negotiating with the devil himself."

"Whew," Hawthorne whistled through his teeth. "Almost an understatement. But it's what Okema would want, if you can pull this off."

Rafe grunted an assent. "If there's any chance, you and wonder boy should try."

Stroking his chin, Jackson shrugged and nodded. "It's true, you are the more powerful of the two, and we've got your back. If you don't succeed, we're not any worse off than before."

"Except." Mato cleared his throat. "We may have to take mad Don and his pack down, if she strikes the hornet's nest."

A sobering thought, and another possible outcome.

Their personal Merlin shifted his ever-changing scrutiny between them. "Many 'ifs' lie before you. Consider my counsel. Seek for your opportunity to act."

Mouth pursed, Jackson inclined his head, then parted his lips. "We shall. What of the vampires we've heard rumors of?"

A burning glow lit Radulf and inflamed his narrowing eyes. "Quite real, and on your trail. They go disguised as wolfmen, yet you can distinguish the difference."

Dread gripped Morgan, and Jackson tensed beside her. "Readily, I should think," he muttered.

"Not so readily." Radulf lifted a cautioning hand. "If I were able, I would accompany you. But I am confined to the hollow. My diminishing powers extend no further. Be ever watchful. And do not neglect the coyotes and their evil queen."

The stilled group seemed to hold its collective breath. Then Jackson straightened with the resolve inherent in him. Again, Morgan sensed why Okema had chosen this young Wapicoli warrior to take his place— why it was Jackson's destiny to become the great white wolf.

"We will watch for anything out of order, any danger that threatens," he assured Radulf, and his shaken pack.

The crow flapped ebony wings, and the wizard stroked its feathers. "Hither Thee Dee grows restless, and our time nears its end. I am not all-seeing, but what wisdom I have I freely impart, and you have my blessing."

He laid one hand on Morgan's head and the other on Jackson's. Energy flowed into her, lessening the heavy fatigue, and bolstering her to better face what lay ahead. "When you leave here in the morning, attune every sense for those who seek you. Make for the Divining Tree. Help awaits you there."

Jackson stirred beneath his palm. "What of the lodge? Wapicoli are gathering and compiling more weapons."

"First, the tree." Radulf was unbending.

"Very well," he agreed, with evident reluctance.

"Though we may have to battle hard to reach it."

"You will." Warning tolled in Radulf's grave assurance.

Foreboding chilled Morgan, like a menacing shadow leering at her. She lifted her eyes to the farsighted wizard. "Will all of us make it to the tree?"

A flicker crossed his expression. "Much depends on you, Morgan Daniel. The fate of all rests with you and Jackson. But especially with you."

She swallowed hard. *As Okema had prophesized.*

"Yet you are not alone. Go with renewed strength in your hearts." He raised his hands over her and the small band. Iridescent light enveloped their circle like rays from heaven.

Lingering questions stilled on her tongue. She soaked in the beneficent stream pouring over her, over each one of them. Starshine bathed her soul. This was better than a knighthood.

Chapter Nine
Whispers—and More—in the Dark

With everything she'd been through today, Morgan should be totally zonked out. Dead to the world. *Sayonara*. Wood popping and settling in the cabin hearth shouldn't have roused her to wakefulness. Yet it had.

Where was a sleeping potion when you needed it? Miriam could brew her one, but the healer was safely tucked up in the lodge with Aunt M., Dilly, Peter, Buck, and Willow, she hoped. Maybe other Wapicoli, too.

The rhythmic breathing and gentle snores from her fellow companions indicated they slumbered soundly. She'd bedded down on the floor in a pile of fur and blankets beside Jackson. The gang slept in shadowed heaps on either side of them, like wolves in a den. Their familiar scent surrounded her.

The fire could use another armful of kindling. No one emerged from their covers to toss it on. Neither did she, snug in her nest. Radulf and Birdie had retired to their small rooms, leading off the kitchen, and the tight knit band had collected in here before the orange glow. Typical pack behavior, she supposed.

Why people assumed wolves were terrified of fire, she didn't know. As long as she wasn't *in* the flames, she appreciated their warmth, as might the family dog snoozing before the hearth. Not that she relished comparing herself to a dog, but canine companions were better than many people.

Caution waved a red flag in her rambling thoughts. Was she awake for a reason?

After Radulf's warning, her watchfulness had heightened tenfold and she listened for anything that didn't belong. The wind no longer whistled beyond the log walls. Maybe the blowing snow had ceased. Better for tomorrow's hike through the white woods. The dangerous trek would soon be upon them.

Too soon.

Jackson was unusually quiet. What was that about?

Rolling onto her side, she met his dark, gold-tinged gaze. "I've heard of sleeping with one eye open. Not two," she whispered.

Propped on an elbow, he gazed into her eyes. "What's your excuse?"

"Do I need one?"

"Suppose not."

They kept their voices low, not wanting to disturb anyone. Heaven only knew what awaited them tomorrow.

Finding Jackson awake and broody wasn't a shocker. He bore a heavy weight, as did she. The awareness of what lay ahead of them, coupled with the maze of uncertainty, tightened her gut. Thanks to Radulf, she felt more empowered to face it now, whatever it might be. The blessing he gave her was one of those moments when a choir should've sung mightily in the background, the missing element in real life adventures—powerful film scores.

She didn't need music to gauge Jackson's mood.

His eyes spoke for him. Likely, hers did too. They were leading their close friends and beloved relations into unavoidable battle, with potentially lethal skirmishes enroute. Their best hope lay in her persuading Uncle Don to side with the Wapicoli—no biggie—he only despised them. And she suspected much more would be demanded of her in fulfilling the prophecy.

Problem was, she could tip the scales toward their success or destruction. Either way.

Jackson curled his fingers at her cheek. "You will prevail, Morgan. I know it."

Goosebumps flushed over her skin at his touch and hushed confidence. "As will you."

A shadow crossed his gaze. "Remember, come what may, you must get them to the tree."

She eyed him closely. *"Together.* We'll get them there together," she insisted, as forcibly as she could without waking everyone up.

His hesitancy was palpable. "You're the most vital one."

Shaking her head, she shushed him. "How can you say that? We're *both* meant to succeed Okema."

Still, he didn't appear convinced. "You've been gifted with the moonstone, have the connection with the Star People, and can draw on the blue energy. If it comes to a choice between us, I'll take the hit. You must go on. Okema wants the survival of the Wapicoli." Again, he caressed her cheek. "He chose well when he summoned you."

She covered Jackson's hand with hers. "He chose well in the seventh to come after him. I cannot do this without you by my side."

His fatalistic expression didn't alter. "You could, if

you had to. Promise me, if I fall, you'll fight for our people."

A molten tide welled within her. Anger, fear of losing Jackson, overwhelming love for him, and determination ignited in a combustible combination. "I promise. But you will not fall. I won't let you. Stop this *if* talk right now, and wipe that 'I'm doomed' look off your face, or I'll wipe it off for you. And don't think I couldn't."

The ghost of a smile curved his lips. "Not for a single solitary second. Your eyes are flashing fire, and you radiate power. I wouldn't want to be the one who crosses you."

"Then don't." She gripped his shoulder. "I refuse to lose you to Panteras, or a coyote witch and her pack, or her demon lizard mother, enemy werewolves, vampires…you name it. We'll survive them all, Jackson Wapicoli. No matter how sinister. You will come into your birthright when Okema determines. And you will be ready for that moment."

"Whew," he whistled under his breath. "I thought I was tough. You kick major ass, Wolf Girl."

"Kick it with me. Or I'll beat the crap out of you."

The widening smile spread to his eyes. "Deal."

Closing her arms around his neck, she pulled him into a kiss both tender and fierce. Thrills rippled through her as he kissed her back, hard and deep, with all the emotion he'd kept hidden these past days. Everything he was, everything he meant to her, even beyond the passion between them, came home to her in the searing kiss. And the physical side of their relationship was an earth-scorching ribbon of flame.

If they weren't surrounded by the pack, they might

lose themselves in each other, and go against Okema's stern warning. He'd decreed no mating before marriage and no marriage before eighteen, or they'd interfere with the darn prophecy, jeopardizing its ultimate end. How, or what that was, she didn't know, but Jackson must have the same awareness amid the desire surging through them. She felt his wanting, and he had to be equally, acutely, aware of hers.

A low groan escaped him, and he pressed heated lips over her cheek, pausing at her ear. "The day after your next birthday, we're getting married."

Exhilarated, almost too winded to reply, she panted. "Not the big day itself?"

"No. Morcant birthdays always fall on a full moon. We don't want to spend our wedding night as wolves running with the rest of the pack."

"True. Bad enough now." They could barely move without bumping Hawthorne or elbowing Jimmy. Fortunately, Batboy could snooze through a zombie attack, if he didn't deem it worth his while to get involved.

Jackson's warm breath tickled her ear. "Not exactly the ideal spot for a make out session."

She lost it, and giggled.

Grunting something unintelligible, Rafe thumped the blanket he'd wadded into a pillow and resettled himself. "Guys, get a room."

Like they could.

Hawthorne lifted his head. "Radulf's or Birdie's?"

Jackson chuckled. "Are we evicting one of them to the loft?"

Morgan surveyed the overhead attic-type space. "Not very inviting. It's murky, cold, and stuffed with odds and ends. Plus, the crow and owl roost up there somewhere."

"Heck. The wizard hangs out in caves with bats," Hawthorne mumbled, flopping onto his side. "What's a loft? We'll probably be camped out in snowy woods tomorrow night."

Mato hunkered in his nest like a hibernating bear. "All the more reason you two had better get some sleep."

At his no-nonsense tone, Jackson exchanged wistful glances with her. "Ten-four, bro."

"Roger that." Tingles skimming her from head-to-toe, she curled with her back against his muscular chest and his strong arms wrapped around her. "Channel all of that passion into staying alive," she whispered, "and you'll do just fine."

He held her close. "You've given me plenty to live for."

She'd give him a heck of a lot more, if she could. Not if—*when*! "Keep the faith."

"And don't get shot, stabbed, bit, torn up, spelled—always gotta watch for that one—mesmerized, maybe. Not sure what all the vamps can do." Jimmy must've decided to take an interest. "Remember, I'll tag. You bag. And Morgan will incinerate 'em."

Jackson ruffled his hair. "Got it, Jimbo."

Batboy never ceased to amaze her.

Jimmy tucked against her other side like a balled up squirrel. "Wish Egbert was ready to ride. Cause when he is, I'm on it..." he trailed off sleepily.

Didn't she know? Maybe the whiz kid was the one who'd get them to the Divining Tree.

****

Come Hell or high water. Or snow, Morgan added to Uncle Don's country saying. Somehow, they'd get through this day.

The freshly powdered woods spread before them in every direction, as they followed Radulf through the forest. Sparkling diamonds covered each leafless limb like heavily frosted cake, and evergreen boughs drooped beneath the weight. All was still, except for an occasional birdcall overhead and fluttering between the high branches. A white flurry descended at the brief disturbance. Otherwise, silence.

Fortunately, Radulf had bound the tops of her boots with strips of wool to keep out the snow, and supplied Jimmy with high-topped, fur-lined moccasins, also well-wrapped. Jackson and the others had the advantage over them with their height. Any more snowfall in addition to this storm and she and Batboy would suffer from wet and cold before arriving at their destination—

What was she thinking? Everyone would probably suffer from something or someone before then.

Radulf towered above her in his wide-brimmed black felt hat, and cloak made of fur pelts. His cascading silver hair and beard shone in the early morning light. The wizard's singular appearance was a combination of Medieval, colonial, and Native American elements. Not only was his dress unique, but no one had his changeable eyes or the protective blue sheen encircling them as he did. The effect was nearly blinding against the glistening white backdrop.

He paused and beckoned her near. "This is where I must leave you, Morgan Daniel." He nodded at Jackson and the other four. "Where we must part ways. I advise you to take the path less traveled. Before I turn back and you continue on your journey, I have something for her that will benefit you all."

The ever-curious Jimmy edged closer. "Is it the *Phial of Galadriel*?"

Morgan gave him a look. "I doubt he has the gift Galadriel bestowed to Frodo containing the light of their most beloved star."

"No, small one. Though this may surprise you." With amusement on his lined face, the wizard reached into the leather pouch slung over one shoulder and withdrew a small gold token suspended from a finely crafted chain made of the same precious metal. Sunlight burnished the gold and the rays from it were radiant.

"For you, Wolf Girl." He slid the brilliant necklace into her gloved hand.

Wonderstruck, she gaped at his gift. It was about the length of her pinkie and the width of her thumb, with a resemblance to an oblong tablet. Images of a turtle, an egg, and a flying bird were carved on the front and surrounded by lines. The shape reminded her of the thumb drive she used to have, but this was created eons before computers existed.

Jimmy squinted at the prize through his glasses. "Whoa. That's old."

"Yeah." The tiny tablet must be pure gold and worth a fortune to an antiquities dealer. How Radulf had come into its possession, she had no idea, nor why he was transferring the amazing find to her.

Every eye was riveted on the minute relic in her palm.

"*Megwich*." Touched by his generosity, but puzzled, she searched his silver—now blue—gaze. "What is it?"

"A *cartouche,* or *shenu, as* it was known in ancient Egypt, inscribed with the symbols for the Star People."

She stared at him openmouthed. "Is there a connection between them and the Egyptians?"

Jimmy pounced. "Did space aliens help build the pyramids?"

The wizard shrugged a fur-covered shoulder. "Some believe this. It is possible. The Star People were here long before that time. Wear the cartouche around your neck with the moonstone, Morgan." He held up his hand before she asked her next question. "Yes. I know they gifted it to you. This, too, comes from them and may help you gain entry when you reach the tree."

She startled. "Wait—entry? Where?"

"To the portal." He spoke as if it were obvious.

Had she tumbled down another rabbit hole—or was she about to? This wasn't possible! Swiveling her gaze to Jackson, she mouthed, 'What the heck?'

Eyes wide, he shook his head. No one in their stunned band seemed to have a clue what Radulf was referring to.

He drew his gray brows together. "Okema should have been more instructive."

Jackson shifted his baffled gaze between Morgan and Radulf. "I've often said that, but he's not a big talker."

Hawthorne snorted. "You think?"

Radulf considered their blank faces. "This may be. Yet he is wise. He must wish you to learn for yourselves." He closed Morgan's fingers around his gift. "Guard this and keep it with you always. The Star People have chosen you. That is clear. Okema also knows."

Lordy, what did that mean?

"They called you. You heard them."

"But I don't want to go to another galaxy." Her heart thudded at the thought and dropped into her churning stomach. "I love earth, my pack, Jackson—"

Radulf clucked impatiently. "A flash through the portal is filled with shooting moons and blazing stars. You will return before you know it."

He spoke as if he'd experienced this celestial ride.

"Yes," the mindreading wizard assured her, with the semblance of an encouraging smile. "Or perhaps, they will come to you."

Was a visit from space aliens supposed to make her feel better?

He firmed his expression. "Embrace your gifts, Morgan Daniel. Lead your pack, Jackson Wapicoli. The rest of you, be strong. Mato, my fondest regards to your mother. *Tanakia.*" After uttering the Shawnee for 'until our paths cross again', he turned away and disappeared into the trees.

Morgan stared after him, or the last place he'd been moments before. "What just happened?"

Jackson closed an arm around her shoulders. "It seems that is for us to discover. And I do mean *us.*"

"Yes. We're with you, Morgan." Hawthorne seemed to speak for them all. Heads nodded, and the pack encircled her protectively. Reaching out their hands, they laid them on her arms like a huddle before the big game.

Jimmy wrapped her middle. "'To infinity and beyond'."

Tears blurred her vision. "I hadn't figured on shooting into space. Or a visit from aliens. I was getting myself psyched up to battle vampires and the usual suspects."

Jackson tightened his hold. "You may get to do both. Better put on the new necklace/portal thingie, and let's head out."

She steeled herself. "I will. Just one more thing I wondered. Why is the Egyptian symbol for the Star People a turtle, egg, and a winged bird?"

"Another question for Okema," Jackson muttered.

If they ever saw him again. *When*, she reminded herself.

Chapter Ten
Come into My Parlor, Said the Spider to the Fly

"Do you get the feeling the trees are listening, and not all of them are on our side?" One of Jimmy's *Narnia* references. He trudged behind Morgan, his breath and everyone else's white in the icy air.

"Yeah." No enemy had declared him or herself. *Yet.* But she had the skin-crawling sensation of being watched. "I wonder if the *White Witch* will make an appearance." Her new name for Eve.

"If she does, she won't be alone." Jackson's reply was so low only a shifter's ears, or Jimmy's, could detect it. As usual, their sub-chief led the way.

"After what Eve pulled, I swear she and her coyotes are going down," Hawthorne hissed. "Just wondering if the vamps are as bad, or worse, than Mateo and his Panteras?"

"Not looking forward to discovering." Rafe's admission pretty much said it all.

Mato rumbled in his throat. "Buck up, guys. We're not pushovers. Maybe they should worry about us."

"That's the spirit." Jackson shot a glance over his shoulder, his smile shadowed beneath the fedora.

Morgan was preoccupied with the whole Star People, possible launch into outer space thing, but this didn't mean she wasn't alert to any movement or sound, however muffled. Sniffing the frigid breeze, she scouted for signs of life beyond the forest creatures. The Divining Tree was still tortured miles away, and they weren't making good time snaking through heavy growth. The track they'd hiked in on yesterday looked good by comparison, and the washed-out road before that, a maintained highway.

Fallen branches often blocked their way. Enormous limbs must be dislodged, gone over, or around—not an option with thorny briars barring each side of the trail at inconvenient intervals. Hedges of mountain laurel also hemmed them in. The evergreen thicket would be a riot of pink blossoms in late spring, but was an annoyance now.

Shifters could run and leap. But Jimmy couldn't keep up, and leaving him behind not an option. Plus, bounding through snow with all these obstacles to cross would take its toll on them in this polar chill.

Sometimes, the path disappeared entirely. Out came the tomahawks, and the guys, except Batboy, chopped a path through the hedge and whacked apart choking tangles of grape vines. Jackson insisted Morgan save her strength for bigger battles.

Now what? A massive tree had snapped and sprawled drunkenly across the trail. Lichens the size of plates sprouted from the moss-encrusted bark like ears.

Itching to see if she could shift it with her blue energy, she lifted her gloved hands. "Let me have a go."

Again, Jackson shook his head. "I'm keeping you in reserve for when we really need you. Besides, the glow might attract attention."

"True." And any attention was unwanted. She knew the drill.

Mato lowered his pack and stepped forward in his thick green canvas coat, his boots leaving large tracks in the snow. Together, he and Jackson heaved the toppled giant and tossed it aside with extra shifter muscle. Mere mortals couldn't have budged it. Even so, their chests heaved.

Frustration welling in her, she gestured at the expanse of wooded whiteness. "This keeps happening. We've been hiking all morning, except for a quick snack." And she wanted more, but they couldn't devour their stash in one sitting. "What was Radulf thinking when he said to take the trail less traveled? Did he mean partway, or until we reach the Divining Tree? We'll be all day and half the night at this rate."

Nodding, Rafe scanned the forest. "We've got to get to the trucks."

"Better hope they run." Jimmy slapped gloved hands against his enchanted fur coat to warm them.

"They will. Mato's a mechanic." Jackson motioned for the pack to huddle up, his expression weighted with the cares of a leader. "We're more likely to be detected in the pickups. Is it worth the risk?"

"It's one we have to take." Hawthorne waved toward the direction of the road. "If we cut across, we should find them. Don't think we've gone too far at this snail's pace. Reaching that doggone tree will be faster in trucks. And warmer. Cubbie's gonna turn into an icicle."

Jimmy parted bluish lips. "Not in my *bunny coat* and wizard moccasins."

"Even so." Morgan wasn't thrilled with an extended sojourn in these cold-to-the-bone woods either. "I figure ambush awaits us either way. We might as well be in pickups when it strikes."

Shaking his head, Mato raised a cautioning hand. "Don't discount Radulf's advice too quickly. What if we hike to the next rise first? The thicket thins out, and we'll have a better view of the road from there. Help us get our bearings."

Jackson considered their wise friend. "Good idea. It's times like this we could use a teleporter to scout ahead."

"Or sideways." Morgan stamped cold feet. "Maybe we should've brought Dilly after all. She pops around like a pinball." The ditzy girl wasn't a warrior, but she had certain skills.

Smiles and grunts of approval greeted her suggestion.

Hawthorne grinned. "I second that." He certainly appreciated Dilly's other attributes.

"Next time." Jackson didn't add, 'assuming there is one.' Resuming the lead, he forged ahead, breaking the trail. He had the hardest job, while Mato carried the heaviest pack.

As far as Morgan could tell, taking this route had done nothing except hamper their progress, unless it helped them evade enemies by concealing their position. Meanwhile, clouds blotted out the sun. The strengthening breeze blew snow in her face and it was flurrying.

All those grueling hours of warrior training on top of her inner wolf helped her journey on and up the next steep incline. She'd slog day and night if she must, but didn't prefer it. Jimmy was one tough kid, but still a kid.

Finally. Jackson motioned for their band to halt.

Clustered together on the rise, the wind blasting them, they peered down through the bare trees and rocks at the road below. Only the evergreens and whirling flakes partly obscured their view.

She pointed at the trucks visible along the verge where they'd left them. "Unbelievable. What are the odds?"

"Non-existent. This isn't mere circumstance. Hold on. Lookey there." Jackson gestured at the movement in the trees near the abandoned vehicles. "We've got company."

Sure enough, men were camped out in potential ambush. Not ordinary males—werewolves. She inhaled deeply, and detected a familiar scent. "Uncle Don and his pack are waiting to surprise us."

Hawthorne leaned forward for a better view. "Not very friendly after Okema let him off with a warning. Maybe Don heard our mighty leader's gone walkabout, and doesn't realize we've got a new one."

"He's not up to speed on Morgan, either." Jimmy's unwavering faith in her was heartening, and a tad unnerving.

Jackson pushed back the stands of dark hair whipping across his face. "We're scenting them from the updraft. They can't detect us yet. To our advantage." He sniffed again. "I'm also picking up the blood musk of something else. Not sure who or what."

"Me too." Morgan nodded. "More baddies down there. I was wrong to doubt Radulf. He must've intended us to see this." Blinking in the fine flakes, she cast an apologetic glance at Mato, then lifted her gaze to Jackson's. "How do we proceed?"

Probably one of the moments their sub-chief had

been dreading. But he squared his jaw. "I'd say there are half a dozen rogue 'weres' with Don. Maybe more. We have Wapicoli warriors, a bearwalker, wonder boy, and the Seventh Morcant." A speculative glint in his eyes, he cupped gloved fingers to her cheek. "What do you think? Want to fly down this hill? It's breezy enough to harness the wind."

She hadn't expected his invitation, and envisioned the feat. "I suppose I could. It'll take all the power I possess. Maybe more."

"This is what I've been saving you for. Your uncle won't expect this. None of them will. Their focus will be on you. The rest of us will silently descend and get into position. We'll have your back."

Low assents echoed his assurance.

"I'm ready." Jimmy patted the paintball rifle slung over his shoulder. "I'll help you negotiate, too, if you need me. But I'd rather plaster him," he added, an edge to his tone.

The kid must still sting from their uncle's scorn, especially considering how much he'd adored the man, a former librarian and outdoorsman who used to take him camping.

She weighed their options. "Both. Be ready to mark them, easier to spot in this white, and help me reason with a madman. If we can't get through to Uncle Don—" She broke off. Everyone knew what this meant.

Empathy warmed Jackson's long glance. "We'll give you and Jimbo a chance to reach him first. But if we have to act, it'll be war."

Heaviness weighed her chest. "Take no prisoners."

"Wouldn't do any good if we did. A captured werewolf isn't gonna side with us. He'll await his opportunity to attack." Jackson clasped her shoulder. "If anyone can reach him, it's you, Morgan."

Pressing her lips together to stop the quiver, she nodded.

Snowflakes swirled past his earnest gaze. "Remember, the Star People have gifted you. No one has your powers. No. Not even me," he added, before she could argue. "Not Miriam. No other Wapicoli or Morcant does. You can do what no one except Okema can. Are you ready?"

It was now, or never. "Yes."

He slid his hand to hers and squeezed her fingers. "All eyes will be on you when you take off. Including ours. Only Jimbo has seen you do this."

And yet, Jackson had faith in her. It shone from his dark eyes unwaveringly. She gazed around the circle. They all believed.

He gave her hand a parting squeeze and stepped back. He'd never looked more handsome, standing tall and proud, the bow over his shoulder, long hair blowing around him. She prayed to be worthy of him, of her pack.

To boost her power, she clasped the moonstone at her throat. The energizing current flowed into her through the gloves. Then she motioned everyone back.

Don't fight the wind, an inner voice directed. *Use it.*

Whether it was the ice queen's, Okema's, or the Star People, she didn't know. Whatever unique gifts had been bestowed upon her, she summoned them now. The blue light charging through her radiated from her fingertips.

Giving herself to the bluster, she circled off the

ground. Round and round she turned in a shimmering spiral. A downward glance revealed the wonder in their upturned faces. But a glance was all she dared. Her focus must be on rising through the trees.

Pine boughs brushed her in a snowy shower. She hadn't ever ascended this high before and refused to allow doubt to jeopardize her ability. No thought for *what if* she suddenly plummeted to the frozen earth. There could be no *if* in this ascent, only *do*.

Passing between the tallest branches, she pushed up with her boots and rose above the topmost tips of the trees. She wheeled in the wind like a bird. The sharp cold knifing through her took her breath away, but she was too exhilarated to care. She was one with the elements, and the woodland scents, with the very essence of the forest.

The wind had one direction and she another. Willing herself toward the road winding through the woods, she circled above the snowy track. Men, their heads upturned, abandoned the hideout among the trees and walked into the clearing. She glimpsed Uncle Don among them, gaping at her as he might a flying saucer. Maybe she shone like one.

She spun lower, out of reach, but close enough to speak. When she landed, she hoped she had enough energy left to defend herself, and scare the bejeebers out of her onlookers. They appeared darned impressed now. Uncle Don stood stock-still, his blue eyes riveted on her, a week old beard roughening his chin. The hooded parka, snow pants, and winter boots he'd camped in were familiar to her, though not this man as he was now. He'd disappeared with one bite. She prayed he was still in there somewhere.

He shook his head, as if to convince himself he wasn't dreaming. "How the blazes did you learn that trick?"

Not the response she wanted. "No trick, Uncle. A gift."

"That so?" Out jutted his bulldog chin. "From who?"

"You don't know them, and won't unless you listen to me."

His hood fell back, revealing dirty blond hair. "You've got my attention, girl. Spit it out."

She hovered above him. "Your enemies are great. Side with the Wapicoli before you face them alone."

A sneer at his mouth, he waved a gloved hand at his fellows. "Do I look alone to you?"

As Jackson had guessed, there were six men, plus Uncle Don. She recognized four from the time they'd invaded the Halloween party at the lodge. She wrinkled her nose at their gamey scent. Had he recruited them from a bar? Not the sort to pledge undying loyalty.

All were armed with knives. No visible guns. Odd. That much, they must've gotten from the Wapicoli.

She eyed the two in back more closely. These men were different. Their headgear, made from wolf pelts, even the wolf's head, was downright primal. And they had a Native American look about their black eyes and dusky skin. Pelts and buckskin clothed them from their coats, tight-fitting pants and leggings, to their high-topped moccasins. They were lean and definitely mean. Cunning, too.

What the heck? Was there another wolf clan somewhere in the wilds? If so, why had they joined this rogue pack? And why had Uncle Don let them in?

Who made headwear out of wolves? Abominable. She wouldn't trust this pair as far as she could throw them, and she hoped it was pretty far.

Something strange about those eyes. The glittering gaze lured her like a spider to its web. Not only drew her, but commanded her focus. The sense that she'd been under such hypnotic influence before returned.

What had Miriam said about *mesmerizing eyes?* She sniffed the blood musk. Radulf's warning beat in her drumming heart.

Wrenching her gaze away, she stabbed a finger at them. "Vampires!"

Chapter Eleven
Fur, Fangs, and Claws

Part women, part wolf, Morgan touched down on the white rutted road. Strands of her blond hair blew in the snow-laced wind, but fire coursed through her veins. She'd shifted enough to harness the wolf, while keeping the advantages of human form. She could melt the flakes with a thought.

Startled men circled her, the vamps better concealing their surprise behind hooded eyes. No retreating now. She planted her boots.

"Deceivers!" With a flip of her fingers, she zapped blue light at the vampires in wolves' clothing. They hurtled backward into the snow banked against a wide tree trunk.

Good. Enough power remained in her to battle the treacherous pair. Like a wrathful angel, she'd come to deliver judgment.

Growls rumbling from his men, Uncle Don rounded on her. "What are you doing, girl? They're one of us!"

"No. They've bewitched you, Uncle." She swept her molten gaze at his pack. "All of you. You can see it in their eyes."

He tilted his head at her as if surveying a rare phenomenon, which she was. "Nonsense. Have you gone mad?"

She gave a dry laugh. "Asks the king of crazy?"

His mouth opened in protest. "Just because I want you, a Morcant, to join my pack?"

"Not only that, and I'm more than a Morcant now. Unless you've met others like me."

"Never in a million—"

"Just a sec." She sent the evil duo scrambling to their moccasins face down in the snow.

"Will you stop?" Uncle Don seized her shoulders and promptly released her. No doubt, the near electric charge running through his hand influenced his hasty action.

"Sorry." She met the exasperation in his once beloved face. "I'm protecting us both from these demons. When did they infiltrate your pack?"

"They *joined* us yesterday."

She inhaled the pungent blood musk, much stronger this close. "Just showed up, did they? How convenient. Take a good sniff and tell me they're true wolves. Only the poor creatures they butchered to fashion those creepola head thingies could make that claim."

He bristled annoyance, and his men weren't receptive to her either. Only the hesitancy in their demeanor kept them from attacking her outright. If they thought they had a chance at winning, they'd be on her in an instant.

She pointed at her resistant relation, light emanating from her fingers. "Must I zap some sense into you? Maybe the crackle will jerk you from this spell you're under."

"*Un moment s'il vous plait,*" a low voice broke in.

The French for 'One moment, please,' uttered in a

strange accent caught her attention.

The older of the two vampires rose, brushing himself off. "Before you zap another, allow me a word, *Fille Loup.*"

Which meant *Wolf Girl*, she pieced together from French class. Did he know her name, or was he going by her rather obvious appearance?

She narrowed what she knew were flaming blue eyes at him. "Shouldn't you be tucked up in a comfy coffin until sundown?"

He fixed his glinting black gaze on her. "*Très-drôle.*"

The phrase translated to *very amusing*. He appeared anything but. "*Excusez-moi.* I'll have to work on my vampire humor. Buffy has a great repertoire to draw from."

"Not necessary on my account, *mademoiselle.*" If he were familiar with the famed vampire slayer, he didn't comment. Probably not a favorite TV series.

She scrutinized this French-inclined blood sucker. His weathered face bore evidence of age, though he could be anywhere from fifty to five hundred. The tinge of yellow in his dark eyes had her leaning toward older, a relative term for vampires. His high cheek bones and slightly flattened, rounded nose were characteristics of some Native American tribes, though she had no idea which ones. Nor was she aware of any vampire tribe or offshoot, let alone one with French associations.

History wasn't her strong point. She recalled some tribes who lived farther north had allied themselves with France during the French and Indian War—over two hundred and fifty years ago. Okema was alive then and might shed some light when he reappeared, or

Miriam. But Morgan was baffled.

Seizing on her momentary uncertainty, the vampire stepped closer and extended an unlovely hand with fingernails resembling talons. "It seems we have had a misunderstanding. Gotten off on the wrong foot," he wheedled, pouring hypnotic rays on her.

She rebuffed his phony attempt at civility and warded off the pull with less effort than it had taken to repel Lilith. "No misunderstanding. By the way, your mesmerizing powers are weaker than the Mountain Witch's."

"That gorgon." He spat the name.

"So you know her?" Morgan hadn't seen that one coming.

The lines in his face tightened. He drew black brows together and he wrinkled his nose. Sheer disdain.

He stabbed a clawed finger at her. "I know much, and you little. This is not the extent of my power."

"Nor is it mine." She prayed hers held out and reinforcements arrived soon.

He pursed thin lips tinged purple, then parted them. "We know of you, Daughter of the Wolf."

Concealing the twinge of alarm, she argued. "Uncle Don told you about me."

The eyes beneath the wolfish headgear never left hers. "No need. The Elder seeks the Seventh Morcant."

Another spasm stabbed her knotted stomach. "Elder? I'm honored. Are you his messengers?"

A wicked smile revealed undeniable fangs to anyone not mesmerized, which ruled out Uncle Don and company. "I am Sitis. This is Deuce." He gestured at his more youthful companion, younger in appearance, anyway. The dude could go back centuries.

His paler features were similar to the spokesman called Sitis, but less pronounced. His fingernails weren't as hooked, so he was less revolting. Apples and oranges, really. Both repulsed her.

Sitis pointed one of his talons at her. "We serve The Elder. He wishes you to do the same. Join us."

She refused to be intimidated. "Who's *us*?"

He thumped his pelted chest in pride. "The *Guerriers*. Warriors from a northern tribe more ancient than the Wapicoli. Mere *bébés*, by comparison." A curl of his lip accompanied this last barb.

Gleaning information was vital. She checked the urge to send him sprawling on his flared nostrils. "Allied with the French, were you?"

Sitis smiled ingratiatingly at her. "Many years ago."

"Yet you retained their name for warrior."

Again, the sardonic smirk. "Easier for converts to pronounce."

"Than what? Mound builders isn't a tongue twister."

He simply eyed her with that fixed gleam.

Not very forthcoming. She tried a more direct approach. "Most tribes were driven west. Why have you come here?"

"Some also journeyed to the far north and lived among the French. As to the Guerriers' reason for coming, our purpose is the same as yours. Hide and strike. Then feed."

She clenched her fists at her sides. "We are not hiding to attack humans."

Scorn lit his eyes. "Will you swear no Wapicoli has ever done so?"

"No," she faltered. "But it's against the rules." She raised her chin. "We are guardians of these mountains."

He shrugged his disinterest in her differentiation between them. "Our homeland is overrun."

"So?" she tossed back. "Isn't that more people for you to snack on?"

He sighed, as though with the weariness of ages. "They have grown wary of us and arm themselves accordingly."

She remembered what Miriam said. "Guns and bullets will not fell you."

"No." A secret triumph curved his purplish lips. "Here, people have forgotten the old ways and the old ones. They foolishly think they are safe."

"With me and my pack around, they are more so."

"Until the hunger overtakes you." He waved aside the retort rising to her lips. "*Pitié*. We hoped you might be persuaded to join us, *Fille Loup*."

She shook her head, her ponytail swishing. "Not this Wolf Girl. And for your information, I'm also a daughter of the stars."

A flicker in his deadpan expression betrayed him. "Ah, *oui*?"

"Oh, yes." She clasped the glowing moonstone, allowing him a brief glimpse of the precious gem. "This came to me. And this." She revealed the golden *cartouche*.

Uncle Don stared from the gifts to her. "Who?" Only the one word escaped him.

"The Star People have chosen me."

A hint of the uncle she'd known touched his eyes. "What does this mean?"

"We shall see."

Situs regarded her narrowly. "You are thrice blessed, Number Seven, and even more dangerous than we knew. If you refuse to join us, the Elder has decreed your death."

"Ah, *oui*?" She feigned indifference. "Get in line."

He waved his talons at the assembly. "All who resist us will perish."

Uncle Don startled. "Wait—What?"

"Your new recruits want me dead, Uncle. You, too, if you get in their way." She hurled fiery energy at Situs and Deuce.

Once more, the two fell back into whiteness. "And now, I'm going in for the kill. You, not I, shall perish."

"We do not die easily. The definition of immortal!" Fangs extended, Situs sprang to hissing life—Deuce behind him.

One moment, the pair were tumbled on the ground, and the next, lunging at her. They moved so fast, she scarcely saw them coming. Had they faked weakness before, tempting her to drain her resources?

Pop! *Pop*! Neon-yellow paint splattered the duo. Jimmy must've reached the trees across the road, which meant the others were with him.

Follow the yellow, an inner voice directed.

While her uncle and the pack gaped at the fight erupting around them, she kicked out, catching Situs in his chest. A split-second revolution, and she thrust her boot into Deuce's belly. Dodging their attempts to smash a fist into her midriff, blacken her jaw, or tear open her throat, she spun away.

She ran up a tree trunk and did a back flip. With the lightness of the snow underfoot, she landed in front of Sitis and sent him backward with a well-aimed kick.

He lunged. She barely avoided those talons. Deuce was on her heels. They were here. There. Everywhere. Rather like Lilith, when the witch had pursued Morgan in her lizard lair.

The neon yellow marking helped her follow their swift movements. She needed a long blade to cut off their heads before they wore her down. Her knife would have to serve. Drawing the blade at her side, she dove at Situs like a soaring hawk and drove it into his chest.

His fowl jaw widened in a howl, and he lurched back. Down he went, slumping on one knee. She had him!

"Not deep enough." He jerked out the knife, slimed in black-red blood, and threw it at her.

She danced aside. "Next time, I'll pierce your shriveled heart!"

Fangs flaring, he and Deuce hurtled themselves at her. Situs knocked her to the ground. Hard. She rolled over, evading his next dive by inches. As she suspected, he was just getting going. He'd been egging her on to deplete her reserves.

Not done yet. She leapt to her feet. Whirling, she unleashed the greatest flash of blue current in her arsenal. One worthy of Okema. A lethal dose. Or it should be.

Situs staggered back, gasping. A noxious combination of scorched death mingled with the blood musk. Deuce doubled over, then toppled onto his side. Were they down permanently?

To be certain, she must let loose another searing flash. But her light was dimming. She rubbed the moonstone. *Nothing*. Only the faintest hum.

She needed to recharge and glimpsed Jackson

rushing at them. *Thank heavens*.

His eyes blazed gold in the flurrying snow. "Choose a side, Morcant! All of you! Now!"

"It better be ours!" More rapid pops and the entire pack were plastered yellow, including Uncle Don. Jimmy's way of encouraging them.

Their uncle spun toward him. "What the devil?"

"Just like you taught me!" Batboy's voice rang from cover, and he plastered Uncle Don's face.

He wiped the sulfurous yellow from his nose and mouth with the rag in his coat pocket. "Our Jimmy did this?" A hint of respect edged his query.

By way of reply, Batboy walked from the trees, blasting away as he went. Snarling men swiped paint from their eyes. Jimmy shouldered his rifle and grasped his bow.

Hawthorne, Rafe, and Mato had shifted into the large gray and tan wolves, and huge brown bear tearing past him.

Pumping his fist, one man shouted, "I say we join the Guerriers! "

"Wrong answer!" An arrow whizzed into his chest from Jackson's bow and he toppled over like a fallen tree.

Enraged men were shifting around her, except Uncle Don. He seemed torn. He wore the look of one fighting to wake from a spell. He must gain his senses, and choose them. Soon. Jimmy had an arrow on the string aimed right at him. His lip tremored, but he'd do it for the pack. She knew he would.

If Uncle Don attacked any of their friends, Morgan would spare the kid and take him down herself.

"Move, girl!" Springing to action, he shoved her

aside.

The stench of death trailing him, Sitis sank his fangs deep into Uncle Don's neck. He must've revived while her back was turned. She should have mustered that second zap!

"No!" Her screams co-mingled with Jimmy's.

Red hazed her mind. Flinging herself on the vampire, she wrenched him off. They rolled over and over, first one on top, and then the other. Wrath twisted his face, and mottled it purple. Her eyes, alone, should have incinerated him to dust.

They didn't, and she lacked enough blue energy to finish him off. Summoning every last ounce of strength she possessed, she sent him flying into the trees. A jagged limb impaled him through the back. Must've missed his heart, dang it.

Panting, she waited for him to shake off the injury—fatal to most. Instead, he writhed on the branch. Then Deuce attacked her with the fury of one devoted to his master. Breath escaped her in a whoosh, and she flattened on her back with him snarling above her. Dreaded fangs neared her throat.

Whistling steel—Jackson swinging his sword. The long blade was the one he'd crafted himself and wore at his side. With a mighty sweep, he sliced off Deuce's head. The gruesome object rolled in the snow, spurting a black-blood trail. She shuddered and scrambled out from under the collapsing body.

One vamp down. One injured. How many besides Sitis remained, and who was The Elder?

No time to consider. Growls, ripping, and tearing converged around her. Fur flew. The packs were colliding.

Jackson pulled her onto her feet. "You all right?"

Chest heaving, she managed a nod. "What about Uncle Don? If not for him that might be me lying there."

Jimmy knelt beside the prostrate man, pressing a wadded cloth to his neck to stem the flow. Batboy, the medic, always had supplies in his pack. Werewolves healed faster than normal humans, but this was a nasty wound. He'd lost a lot of blood. And the vampire who'd dealt the bite was ancient. Who knew what venom his fangs might inflict?

They couldn't lose the uncle they'd only just reclaimed.

"Morgan. Look." Jackson pointed through the whiteness at the oncoming black car.

Gut-twisting memory returned of the monster car from their encounter on the mountain, when she'd been forced over the side. "Panteras. And not our allies. They must've driven past here seeking us and doubled back."

"Mateo could be with this bunch." Jackson waved at their pack. "We've got to go! Get in the trucks now!"

Together, they ran to the spot where Jimmy bent over Uncle Don. His blood spattered the teary-eyed boy.

"We're out of here, Jimbo. I'll get him." Jackson slid his arms beneath the heavier man and lifted him. The werewolf in Uncle Don, coupled with Jimmy's ministrations, had stanched the flow at his throat, but he'd gone pale beneath the streaks of paint and blood. His eyelids didn't even flutter. Not good.

Praying he lived, Morgan bounded with Jackson and her brother to one of the snow-covered pickups. Mato, transformed to human form again, slid into the driver's seat. Jackson hoisted Uncle Don inside and sat cradling him. Jimmy scooted in, and she squeezed beside them.

From the corner of her eyes, she saw Rafe and Hawthorne dash to the other truck. Men and wolves, some lifeless, others wounded, were scattered on the snow. Their pack had dealt the rogue wolves a blow. How many injuries the guys had sustained, she didn't know. Mato had some scratches on his face and blood ran down his cheek. Thank God everyone made it to the vehicles. He turned the key. Engines revved up.

Sitis staggered to the roadside. The old devil must've freed himself from the broken limb. Vampires also had amazing rejuvenating powers, but were they enough for what was coming?

She stuck her head out the partly unrolled window. "How do you do against Panteras?" she yelled, as they sped off.

Chapter Twelve
Wishing Won't Get You There

"Faster, bro!" The big bearwalker drove like mad at Jackson's urging.

Morgan smacked sideways into the truck door. Jimmy crunched next to her, and Jackson gripped Uncle Don, slumped against him. It was utter insanity to tear over the road in these conditions, but what choice did they have?

Either they flee like prison escapees, or stop and face armed Panteras. Quite possibly, the baddest one of them all. *Mateo.*

The name, alone, sent a ribbon of dread through her. *Not now, please Lord.* She wasn't ready for that high voltage showdown yet.

Out in front, Rafe steered and Hawthorne rode shotgun in the blue truck rounding the curves ahead of them. The make of vehicles meant nothing to her, only power, and the beast from the lodge ate up the snow-covered road. They ploughed closely behind 'Big Blue' in Mato's rusty orange pickup, everyone crammed in beside him.

Frowning beneath his fedora, Jackson glanced from the ominous car steadily gaining ground to Morgan. "We'll fight, if we must. But I sure would like you to recharge first."

"Me, too. Wish I knew how, besides rest, which we

haven't got time for. You think Mateo and his pals took Sitis and the rest of the wolves out?" She was puzzled as to why the car hadn't slowed as she'd expected. "They could've gunned down the wolves, but not Sitis. Plus, we heard no shots."

"Assuming Mateo's with the gang on our tail?" Jackson shrugged a broad shoulder. "Maybe he blew past the party we exited to catch the bigger prize. Us. And maybe Sitis pulled a disappearing act."

"Vampires can." Jimmy spoke in a flat voice, his sad gaze on Uncle Don.

He was fading. His ashen face said as much. She didn't need to feel his pulse to detect the weakening heartbeat. Without the maniacal gleam and snarl he'd worn as a recently gone-crazy werewolf, he now appeared much the same as the man who'd been like a father to her and Jimmy. He'd helped his sister, their Aunt M., take care of them after both parents were killed in a car wreck. Not an accident, she'd later discovered, but one perpetrated by city Panteras—the same monsters closing in on them again.

She sighed. "Sitis probably lived to fight another day. He's hung on for untold centuries. We've got to get to the Divining Tree. It's our best chance of survival and the only hope for Uncle Don. I just know it."

Jackson thumbed behind him. "We can't lead them there."

"No." She shuddered at the thought of Panteras defiling the sacred site.

"Got an idea." Jimmy lifted his gaze, a newfound light in his eyes. "Change places with me, Morgan. I'm gonna need the window seat."

She eyed him skeptically. "What are you up to?"

He patted his paintball rifle. "Watch and learn, grasshopper."

"Careful," she grunted, as he squirmed over her and she slid next to Jackson. Sometimes, Jimmy got cocky.

"Safety first. That's my motto."

She snorted. "The heck it is. They have guns, too, remember. Real ones."

A staccato blast confirmed her warning.

"Everyone get as low as you can." Jackson reached across her and jerked the boy down. "It's too big a risk to take."

Batboy thrust out his chin from his hunkered position. "I'm quick and a good shot. I can do this. They won't be able to see where they're going."

Mato scanned the relentless car in his rearview mirror. "Worth a try, Jackson. I'll say when the kid fires."

He gave a reluctant nod. "Pull the hood of that charmed coat over your head, Jimbo, and be ready to duck."

Jimmy did as he said. Snaking out a hand, he unrolled the window. A gust of flurry-laden wind blew into the truck. "Ready when you are."

Another round of shots ricocheted off their tail gate. The truck rocked and they braced for more. She hated this.

Mato signaled Batboy. "They spun on that last curve. The shooter's knocked off balance. Go for it."

Jimmy stuck his head out the window and blasted away at the windshield behind them. Yellow goo spattered the glass, the thickest patch blotted in front of the driver.

He crowed. "They can't see crap until they clean this off. Wait—"

The blotched car veered right and Morgan glimpsed the all-too familiar face glaring at them from the passenger side window. A sneer revealed the gold outlining Mateo's white teeth, and his tawny eyes were glow-in-the-dark. Kind of like the yellow paint. His oily musk reached her on the breeze. Noxious. Worse, he aimed the gun in his hand right at her.

Jimmy fired first. Sulfurous globs plastered Mateo's eyes, nose, and mouth. The Pantera leader's bullet launched aimlessly overhead, while Batboy didn't miss a single splat. Only when the redecorated car ran off the road into the trees, did he ceasefire.

Jackson gave a low whistle. "Pin a medal on superkid."

"Thanks, Captain." Jimmy didn't pause to gloat. He was intent on Morgan. "We could get them. Do you have any power back yet?"

She had the same urge to go after Mateo and his gang, while they were shaken up and temporarily stuck. But Uncle Don needed immediate care. And the truth was, she didn't.

"No. We've got to get to the tree. But I promise you, the next time we have the chance, Mateo is going down."

Luminous gold fired Jackson's eyes. "I second that."

Mato rumbled in his throat. "We're all on board. The dude's walking the plank. I'm wondering what these Star People are gonna do for us?"

So was Morgan. "I don't know. But Radulf said to go."

Jimmy settled back in his seat. "And if they turn out to be like the not-so-good aliens in *Signs*?"

Not a happy thought.

"Tinfoil hat time," he muttered.

Jackson rubbed his chin. "I'd say we return to the lodge and see what Grandma Miriam can do for Don. But as Morgan's so sure the Star People have the answers and can heal…"

It was all she could do not to flounder in reply. "They've called me. Given me these gifts. It must be for something good."

"Agreed." The bearwalker was faithful.

"All right." Jimmy laid his rifle on the floor. "Won't be needing this for a while, I guess."

"I wouldn't count on it." Jackson resettled their failing uncle against him. "If you're wrong, Morgan. He's a goner." The death scent hung over him.

She couldn't believe she was choosing the unknown over the familiar lodge and dearest Miriam, their wise healer and mentor. Help surely awaited them there. But Radulf had specifically said to go to the tree first, and he'd emphasized the fate of the mission ultimately rested with her.

Obedience wasn't her strong point, but she didn't dare go against the farsighted wizard. He'd proven himself and deserved her trust. "To the tree, Mato. It's what Radulf wants."

"Right you are, my lady." He gestured at Rafe to go on.

"We better be sure they understand. I'll signal them. Here, take Don." Jackson shifted the unconscious man into Morgan's arms.

He sagged heavily in her grasp, weighing her heart.

Jackson held up his right arm, five fingers raised, and slid his left forearm beneath it from left to right. Then twisted his hand, like a tree blowing in the wind. He dipped his eyes to hers. "Sign language."

"Right." A lot of signs came from the Native Americans, she recalled.

Rafe gave him a thumbs up.

Hawthorne turned and lifted his hands in the universal gesture for, 'What's happening?'

Morgan knew he was asking about Uncle Don. Jackson shook his head. No one needed a translator for what this meant. He gathered her limp uncle back into his secure hold. Bumps in the road and swerves didn't dislodge him.

He was so still. What if they were too late to save him?

The full realization of what he meant to her flooded back. Tears rolled down her cheeks and sobs rose in her throat. "Please don't die, Uncle. Stay with us. We're here for you."

Maybe some power was left in the moonstone. Rubbing the gem for whatever it might give her, she laid her other hand on his slumped head. Faint energy flowed through her fingers. She willed the beneficial stream into him. "I'm sorry for the hurt between us. I need you back. Whatever strength I have, let it flow into you, and give you new life. Draw power from me."

"And me." Moisture filled Jimmy's eyes and wet his freckled cheeks. He laid his small hand on Uncle Don's broad shoulder. "Please live, like you taught me. We are the last males of our line."

Jackson clasped his other shoulder. "Don Morcant, as the Wapicoli alpha, I welcome you into our clan.

Join us and fight by our side. May old wounds between the Morcant and Wapicoli be healed, and let there be peace. Live, now."

Morgan had never loved Jackson more.

Agonizing seconds passed with no change. Uncle Don still sagged in his hold.

What more could they do? She was sending every bit of energy she had into him. Withholding nothing. They'd beseeched him, and Jackson had practically ordered the fading man to live. Keeping their hands in place, they continued in fervent silence while Mato drove.

Snowy trees passed as the truck wound toward the clearing where the oak stood. White-tailed deer bounded away on long legs. Wild turkey flapped from the underbrush, their boldly barred wings and red heads standing out in the flurries.

Above their gobbles, she heard the stone hum. The noise it emitted was louder than before. Not ear-splitting, more of a homing signal?

Morgan Daniel, we await you.

She jerked around. "Did anyone else hear that?"

Jackson slanted his eyes at her. "Do we ever?"

"Tell them to put us on speaker phone." Jimmy sniffed and swiped his nose on the crumbled cloth in his hand.

"What the?" Jackson nudged her. "Look."

The tiniest hue of color had returned to Uncle Don's pallid face. He stirred slightly and opened lips now tinged with flesh tones. "We are nearing them."

How did he know? She exchanged widened glances with the others, then gazed back down at her uncle. Life was seeping back into him.

Grateful, mystified, she braced herself for what lay ahead. She suspected they all did.

Chapter Thirteen
'Not All Who Wander Are Lost'

What now? And where were those space aliens?

Unvoiced questions hung in the cold air. Even after witnessing Uncle Don's miraculous revival, Morgan didn't entirely trust these unknown beings; neither did the pack. The hushed woods reflected their watchful silence. No birds called in the muffled forest. All was quiet except for the hum at her throat from the moonstone.

Was the lack of activity related to their arrival?

Small animals took cover when they detected the presence of a great horned owl or other predator. Surely, the Star People weren't considered a threat? Maybe it was their band. She'd never heard the woods this muted, and the silence was eerie.

They walked through the snowy stillness toward the clearing, Uncle Don leaning on Jackson's support. He hadn't regained full strength yet. Even so, he was putting one foot in front of the other.

Had the Star People aided him because of her, Jimmy, and Jackson's petition, or for some other reason? They'd played an essential part in his recovery, she was certain. Granted, he'd been a pretty bad werewolf, but was changing for the better when Sitis bit him. Maybe they deemed him worthy of saving. Whatever their code, they hadn't left him behind.

The wary pack's muted tread led them into the perfect circle in the woods. She caught her breath. There it was. *The Tree*. Splendid, despite its flaws, it rose from the center of the clearing.

Lightning had struck the ancient oak many times, and the trunk was bent, but the tree had survived. Thrived, even. One massive limb pointed toward the spot where they'd paused—where The Star People had landed over two centuries ago. Okema had notched the surrounding trunks with the sign of an arrow to signify the sacred site. The snow hid many of these markings now. No matter. They knew where they were, except for Uncle Don, the new initiate in the group. It was *why* they were here that eluded them.

Anticipation welled in her, the sense of expectation palpable in the pack. What was it Radulf had said about the *cartouche*, that the Egyptian relic might help her gain entry? To what?

They scanned the trees circling the perimeter like sentinels. These stately watchers held no interest for them. All eyes fixed on the giant oak, its spreading branches laced white in the lightly falling snow. Hushed moments passed...

Nothing stupendous happened. Shouldn't there be some sort of signal? A sign? Not this shrouded emptiness.

Jackson closed his free arm around her, the other still supporting Uncle Don. "I think they're waiting for you. Remember, to gain insight from the Divining Tree you must lay your hand on its bark."

Her heart fluttered. A host of butterflies could've taken flight in her chest. "Okay. Sure." She had no better idea.

He tightened his hold in an embrace, then released her. "Go on. We're here."

Why was she forever heading off on these adventures by herself? At least, it felt this way. She couldn't deny the fact that she was the one they'd called. Dang it.

Doing her best to conceal jangling nerves, she nodded. There was no way forward except to leave Jackson, leave them all, and go it alone to the ginormous oak. She hoped wearing gloves didn't matter because she was darned cold and not taking them off. Her one rebel move. Kind of lame.

Clasping the furrowed bark with her left hand, she took the golden *cartouche* in her right hand and held it out. "I'm here. Show me what you will."

The words had scarcely left her lips when a brilliant light blazed through the whiteness from high overhead.

What the heck?

Had the tree acted as a transmitter? Maybe it, the moonstone, and the *cartouche* worked together? She tucked the gold token back beneath her jacket.

Adrenaline surging in her, she shaded her eyes with one hand and gazed upward. Flurries wet her lashes. The others did the same. The glow was as bright as all the stadium lights at a football game combined into one beam. Seeing anything clearly was impossible, even with her superior wolf sight.

Wait—she detected the glint of silver. Something was up there. Stumbling out from under the tree, she strained for a better look. A disc-like object hovered above them.

Holy crap. A flying saucer. The long-awaited Star

People had come at last, and Miriam was missing it.

Morgan wanted to shout the news and run fast and far at the same time. Then a tractor beam seized her. Blinking in the radiance, she twisted to break free. There was no escape. The ray gripped her like a bear trap, and she could probably pry one of those apart and get away. Not from this.

Images revolved around her. Jackson's stunned eyes. Jimmy's shock. Uncle Don's wonder. Hawthorne, Rafe, and Mato gaped at her. Everyone seemed frozen in place. Normally, nothing phased Batboy. He was stumped now.

Jackson bounded to life. "Morgan!" His cry reverberated through the pack.

Shifting Uncle Don to Mato's support, he lunged forward. Arms outstretched, he fought to reach her. She strained toward him. Their fingers brushed as he whizzed past, but he wasn't the one whirring around. She was. Then she lifted off the ground, and not by her own will. A force beyond her wind flying ability lay behind the propulsion. This power exceeded anything she'd ever known.

Jackson sprang up, up, up, and grasped her legs. The field holding her threw him off. He tumbled to the ground. Hard. It seemed these beings desired an audience with her, and her alone. He'd better be Okay, or they'd get an earful.

Could her heart possibly thud any louder?

Thank God. He was standing—no—climbing the tree. Was he trying to intercept her? He couldn't possibly succeed. Even if he grabbed her, the force field would toss him again. But she admired his never say die efforts.

She waved at him to stop. "I'll be back!" On that, she was determined.

Strange thoughts racing through her mind, she rose higher. Did they serve dinner on flying saucers? She was famished. How long would she be gone? Would Jackson and the others wait for her? They couldn't hang out in the woods for hours. They'd have to pitch camp. Everyone was cold and hungry, and Uncle Don still needed care.

Radulf had better be right about this *brief* jaunt into space. She'd trusted him with her life.

Still revolving, she continued her ascent. No snowy boughs brushed her in passing, as she was in the clearing. She soon arched above the trees. Voices shouted her name in the whiteness. Those on the ground must be frantic about her. She glimpsed Jackson perched on the highest limb of the oak. There was nothing he or any of them could do for her, except wait and see. And pray. Her entire spirit was a prayer.

So bright. She reached the metallic-looking bottom of the spaceship, encircled with lights.

The door parted soundlessly in the center, and she found herself inside the craft. *Wowee*. Control panels emitting a blue-green glow spanned much of the compartment. The high tech features reminded her of a pod-shaped flyer from a sci-fi movie.

What was she thinking? Her life was a sci-fi movie.

The knobs, dials, buttons, and switches she expected to see were absent. These were little more than gizmos to her, anyway. Jimmy was far more adept at figuring out their functions. He might not know what to do with the advanced technology, but he'd dive right in. An hour tops, and he'd fly this baby.

Where did the pilot sit? She couldn't tell from her vantage point. Spaceship style doors led off in different directions. She must be in one of several compartments. If they had a deck, or bridge, like on *Star Trek*, this wasn't it.

Whoa. A figure in a silvery robe appeared before her. *Materialized,* unless he'd been there before and she hadn't noticed. Not likely. He—she sensed he was male—was humanoid in shape.

Wizard flashed through her mind upon seeing the robe, but the face peering at her from the hood resembled a wizened tortoise. Not in every detail. Near enough. This explained the turtle carved on the *cartouche.* To ancient Egyptians, these beings must've been the turtle people. Funny, Okema never mentioned the similarity. He'd left a lot unsaid, though. Miriam had too, unless she didn't realize. Also, unlikely.

Were all the occupants of this craft turtle-like? Only the one stood before her. His lidless red eyes, ringed with green, had a timelessness about them. The dusty ages were etched in his lined face, ending in a sort of beak. Maybe younger members of his species didn't appear as though they'd witnessed the creation of the world.

He inclined his tortoise-shaped head beneath the cloak and bent his nearly non-existent shoulders in a bow. "Greetings Daughter of the Wolf and Stars. Welcome Seventh Morcant. We have awaited your coming." He laid a partly webbed hand over his chest, or what she assumed was his chest, possibly his heart. "I am Ahmose."

The similarity to Egyptian in his name struck her as

significant. Which came first, him or the name?

Probably him, and the name followed. This dude could've overseen the building of pyramids, or provided the floor plans.

Bowing in imitation, she laid one hand over her heart. "Greetings Ahmose. I, Morgan Daniel, *earthling*," she emphasized, "and Seventh of my line, am honored to meet you."

"As I am you. Follow me, Morgan Daniel. We will sit together and speak." His fluid voice belonged on the radio. "This way, please."

He was all civility, down to his webbed toes. Gliding, rather than walking, his iridescent robe covering what passed for sandaled feet, he led her to the corner intended for conversing. He paused and waved her into one of several scooped out, egg-shaped seats. The smooth white material comprising them probably hadn't yet been invented on earth.

She lowered herself uncertainly into the seat, pleasantly surprised when it molded to her shape. An exact fit. And the temperature in the compartment was ideal, as if adjusted for her. What temperature turtle people needed, she had no idea.

An armrest emerged at her side bearing a silver cup with a spout. Hey, an unusually posh sippy cup so she wouldn't spill.

He settled his robe-draped self in the chair beside her. "Please, drink."

She was thirsty. What on earth would it taste like? Nothing earthly at all, she supposed, and lifted the cup to her lips. She took a tentative sip.

Ahhh. If moonbeams brewed into sweet nectar with the airiness of a midnight sheen were possible, this was the stuff, and so warming. Her chill dissipated, and her sharp hunger was sated as she imbibed the food and beverage combo.

Wiping her lips on the snowy cloth provided beneath the cup, she sighed. "Delicious. Thank you. Will you have some?"

"No." His robe slid back, revealing a thin wrinkled arm. He could use the extra calories, but waved her aside. "My apologies. This is only a short visit."

She searched his green-ringed reddish gaze. A black line ran across the center of each pupil. "I'm not traveling through a worm hole like Radulf, am I?"

The hint of a smile crossed his aged visage. "Radulf had more time and no anxious friends awaiting his return."

She took another swallow. "He said it was a brief journey."

"Brief is a relative term. He was gone a month in your time. Can your people spare you for this long?"

"Oh my gosh. No." She was vastly relieved to give that particular trip a pass. Sitting in a spaceship with Ahmose, the turtle person, was quite enough to absorb.

She relaxed a little more. "Did you heal Uncle Don?"

He shook his cloaked head. "You did, with the help of your brother, Jimmy, and Jackson. Each are also the Seventh of their lines. You begin to see what lies within Jimmy, the Morcant male of your generation."

"Yes." There was far more to Batboy than she'd realized.

"As for Jackson," her host continued. "Well, you know what is to come to him."

"Not entirely," she admitted.

"Nor does he, or the gifts he already possesses. Power is inherent in each of you. We gave you this."

"We?" She saw no others. "How many are onboard?"

"Only three on this craft, more of a pod, really."

"Yeah. I noted the shape. But it seems plenty big to me."

A slight smile curved his creases. "We have a far larger ship where more of our people await us. Others are also sent out on missions."

Jimmy would love it when he heard about the Mother Ship. "Have you a home planet?"

"Certainly. Odessa is not destroyed. Your astronomers simply have not yet discovered it, but the name is familiar on earth. Many of our names are common there."

Were they speaking Odessian without realizing it?

A question puzzled her. "How do you know English?"

"I am the Odessian Ambassador. I speak all languages."

"Of course." She tried to wrap her mind around sitting in a spaceship/pod with the Odessian ambassador.

He pressed his partly webbed hand to his lined brow, as if the cares of the galaxy weighed heavily upon him. "Many matters require our attention. Some plans go awry. Much remains to be accomplished." Tilting his head to the side, he regarded her. "Our time together is short, Morgan Daniel. I have a gift to aid you in your battle with the vampires."

She sat up straighter. "We were ignorant of their existence until recently. Are they poisonous?"

"Like striking cobras. The Elder carries the deadliest venom in his bite. Guerriers are an ancient vampirian order. They will overrun the mountains. Cities will follow. Unless you stop them."

Crap. "We will. What gift have you for me?"

"The cure." He withdrew a cylindrical vessel from inside his robe, sealed at the top, containing a shimmering blue liquid.

A high tech medicine bottle with an herbal brew from another planet? *Awesome.*

He passed the sphere into her hand. "Your uncle will need three drops to erase all effects of the poison. The bite from Sitis is bad. Others bitten will require six drops, perhaps more. The dosage depends on the victim's size and strength, and who delivers the bite. Twelve drops for the Elder."

A shadow passed over her at his name, and she clasped the precious sphere to her chest. "What if I break it?"

"You will not. You will keep it safe. The evils in your world are growing, many unseen by mere humans. You are more empowered to fight them than any other."

She opened her mouth in protest. "I can't battle alone. What about Jackson?"

"Never fear. He is coming into his inheritance and has an important part to play. Yet, even he, is not as gifted as you. Though he will grow in strength."

A vital name rose to her lips. "Okema?"

The lidless scrutiny intensified. "Okema is like no other in your world. He was forged by fire, and by us."

Hope inflamed her. "Please. Can you tell me where he is?"

"I could. But your part is not yet dependent on

him."

Her inner flame dwindled. "When?"

"You shall see soon enough. Your mission: return to the others with a better understanding of your enemy, and the elixir we have given you. The drops must be dispensed within an hour of a bite or death will follow. Do you understand?"

"All too well. What about Mateo and the Panteras?"

"Evil walks the mountains in various guises." There were no windows in the compartment, but Ahmose waved his hand as if to encompass the ridges. "If you do not halt the darkness, it will spread far and wide. Take heart. You have friends to help you fight this battle, and your uncle, aunt, and brother."

A light glowed in his reddish gaze. "Jimmy is the most extraordinary Morcant male we have ever observed. And so young."

"Are you watching us?" A rather unsettling thought.

"Of late. We track you through the moonstone. You have heard my voice."

She startled. "That was you?"

He inclined his head.

She had to admit, he'd aided her. She pulled out the *cartouche*. "And this?"

"Ah." A smile flickered in his aged face. "Radulf gave you a very special gift in the *cartouche*. When the time is right, it will open a gateway in the Divining Tree itself."

"To where?"

Ahmose gestured above them. "Beyond the stars. Odessa."

Realization dawned. "The portal is there?"

"Yes."

Her heart flopped like a fish out of water. "I really don't want to go."

His expression was grave. "The journey is not for you, Morgan Daniel, but one dear to you."

Fear chilled her. "Who?"

"I cannot yet say how the blow will fall." He shook his head. "Or to whom."

Morgan inhaled sharply. "A fatal blow?"

"Without our aid, death is certain." He pointed at the sphere in her grasp. "That will not be enough to heal this."

Chapter Fourteen
What's in the Egg?

"Place the healing vial inside this, and it will never break." Ahmose handed Morgan a silvery pouch made of unknown material that hung from a strap.

To her eye, it resembled the buckskin pouches Jackson and other Wapicoli wore suspended over one shoulder, or attached to their belts, only this was fashioned by partly webbed hands. Unless, not all Odessians looked the same as Ahmose.

"Thank you. For everything." She tucked the bluish sphere into the pouch. The flap secured seamlessly with invisible space-age tape. She slid the strap over her shoulder and gave the pouch a pat. "There. All safe. I'm ready for departure."

Should she shake his hand? Bow, as before?

Uncertain regarding protocol for bidding farewell to an Odessian ambassador, she nodded her appreciation and turned to position herself above the hatch for her descent to the clearing. "The others must be very anxious about me."

"Doubtless. But I have another gift."

"Really?" *Of course*. Ahmose wasn't the sort to kid around. "You've given me so much already. We can never thank you enough."

"Who is to say what is too much for the giver to give?"

No arguing with his logic. She pivoted to find him cradling an egg in both hands and extending it to her.

Her jaw dropped. It wasn't the size of the egg so much, as the unusual hue. Stardust was the closest she could come to describing the silvery blue, glistening sheen. The exquisite oval was about the size of an ostrich egg, but she hadn't seen one of those up close to be sure.

He smiled faintly at her amazement. "The creature who will hatch from this is named Manetoh."

A warning tolled in her mind, and she stiffened. "Isn't that Okema's name? And doesn't it have to do with a poisonous snake?"

"Yes, Manetoh is also his Shawnee name. But no venomous serpent will come from this."

She relaxed her taut spine. "Good. What is it? Some kind of bird? I remember one carved on the *cartouche*."

"Ah, the *cartouche,* made long ago by the Egyptians to symbolize our people. You saw a great turtle on it, yes?"

"I did." He must not be sensitive about the comparison. Not that there was anything wrong with turtles.

He stroked the iridescent shell. "You also saw an egg?"

She nodded, mutely agreeing.

"The winged creature depicted on the *cartouche* is not a bird, Morgan Daniel."

"No?" She was stumped. "What else could it possibly be? A space creature?"

"Yes. In your world, it is called a dragon." He patted the egg. "That is what laid this."

She stared into his green-ringed reddish gaze. The black line across his pupils didn't flicker. He was in earnest, as if he'd be anything else.

Biting back '*Seriously*?' she attempted a coherent question. "An Odessian dragon?"

"Certainly." He straightened his shapeless shoulders with an air of pride. "It is the decision of the council to entrust you with this rare gift."

"Me?" she gulped. "But—"

He hushed her. "Not only you. Also your pack. You need more help in battling the evil forces rising against you."

Visons of a fire breathing monster rose before her. Not her idea of assistance. "Jimmy's training the thunderbird."

His reddish eyes glinted approval. Jimmy was a favorite. "Manetoh will also require training. The young Morcant will be of aid, and is worthy indeed. And your alpha leader, Jackson, also highly favored, and his cousin, Hawthorne, are familiar with instructing winged creatures."

Hawks, owls, and crows. She could hardly believe she was discussing dragon care. "How big will Manetoh grow?"

"Not terribly large. The size of a big thunderbird."

Could be worse, she supposed, remembering drawings she'd seen of dragons in comparison to puny humans. "Big enough to fly on, if someone dared?" She knew the very person, or persons, who'd dare.

"Exactly. Manetoh will carry you, defend you, and deliver messages."

She squinted at him. "How?"

Ahmose considered her as if she'd missed the

obvious. "He will understand what you want, because you will teach him."

"Right." However that worked. The others had better know.

"He communicates in cries and chirps, similar to a bird."

"I see." She hesitated to pose her next question. "Does he, will he, breathe fire?"

"Yes. This requires special training or he will toast your toes." He transferred the egg into her shaky grasp. "Guard your prize. Odessian dragons are highly sought after."

She clutched the unlikely gift to her middle. "How long until it hatches?"

"*He* will emerge from the shell in three to six days. Take the egg to the healer, Miriam." Ahmose seemed to be on a first name basis with them all.

"Yes. Okay." So Miriam was also a dragon expert? That didn't surprise her as much as she might have thought.

"Manetoh must have warmth," he emphasized. "She will place him in the hearth."

Morgan startled. "Wait—in? Don't you mean beside?"

Ahmose shook his turtle-shaped head. "Miriam will know what is best to do. She is descended from us."

"Yes. She told me. Jackson is also a descendant, and his father, Peter. And on back, I suppose. But..." How did one tactfully observe that none of them looked the least bit Odessian? Nor could she imagine the attraction, even in the distant past, any Wapicoli girl might've had for a turtle-like being.

Amusement crinkled his eyes. He tapped his chest. "You wonder why her ancestor would mate with a male such as me?"

Heat flooded her cheeks. She hadn't meant to be so transparent. "I can't deny the thought has crossed my mind."

He snorted. "I am three thousand years old. The younger of my species are more *appealing*, as you would say. We also have a useful mating tool that aids us in our wooing."

Curiosity overwhelmed her. "What?"

He emitted an undeniable chuckle. "We disguise ourselves as human."

She couldn't seem to keep her jaw from sagging.

"We alter our appearance as we wish. But enough about us. Time wanes. Danger does not. We have a galaxy to patrol, and you, your piece of earth. Foes are many. Defenders few."

He drew a long strip of filmy gauzy stuff from his robe. "Wrap the egg in this to keep it warm."

Taking the inadequate-looking cloth, she wound lengths around her prize and tucked in the ends. She'd made a tidy job of it, if she said so herself, but doubted the cloth would withstand her frigid descent, or the cold forest.

She drew her brows together. "Wouldn't something thicker be better?"

He huffed under his turtle like beak. "This fabric has the strength of a thousand spider webs and transmits the warmth of hot coals. You must trust me."

She cradled the egg like a diapered infant. "I'm sorry. I will try."

A nod of acceptance indicated he was appeased.

"After Manetoh hatches, tie the cloth around his middle and use it as a training leash. See he has plenty of food, and keep the thunderbird from devouring him before he grows large enough to defend himself. I expect they will become fast friends."

She hoped the hissing bird agreed, or that Jimmy could persuade him. "If we have any other questions?"

But Ahmose was gone. Was he a teleporter, too?

The hatch doors opened and she entered the brilliant stream of light. "Until we meet again, Morgan Daniel."

His farewell trailed after her in the swirling snowflakes. "Tell Jackson we are watching him grow in strength and are well pleased."

"Yes!" She had a wealth of information to share with him and the others.

The cutting wind swept her in dizzying revolutions as she hugged her prize. Her immediate goal: reach the ground with the egg intact, not resembling *Humpty Dumpty* after he fell off a wall.

No more than forty minutes could have passed since she'd risen above the clearing, but it seemed longer. When she arrived on the ship, she hadn't even heard of Odessa. Now, she was returning with a cure for vampire venom and a dragon egg. Not bad work for her first trip.

Darn. She should've asked how long it took baby dragons to grow up. Maybe Miriam knew.

Neither Manetoh nor Egbert could help in their upcoming battle with Mateo and his Panteras, or any other enemies. But someday, they'd take to the skies, shrieking, eyes flashing, breathing fire, the Odessian dragon and the Native American version of the winged terror. Fighting for the Wapicoli.

Then she remembered what Ahmose said about her needing the *cartouche* to open the portal and send a mortally wounded loved one to Odessa, and she hugged the egg tighter.

Chapter Fifteen
'Out of the Frying Pan into the Fire'

Guard the egg, repeated in Morgan's weary mind. Fatigue overcame her on the journey back to the lodge on the winding snow-covered road. Bounding from one herculean feat to the next took its toll on a girl, even if she was the Seventh Morcant.

Cradling her charge, she leaned on Jackson in the pickup. Uncle Don slumped on his other side, and Jimmy scrunched against the door, too stoked to sleep in the presence of an actual dragon's egg.

Jackson nudged her. "We're here."

"Thank God." She lifted her head from his shoulder.

Treacherous road conditions had slowed their return to the lodge. Fortunately, the need to drive with reckless abandon had been removed by Jimmy's accuracy with the paintball rifle. No further sightings of Mateo and his Panteras, Sitis and the vamps, or others among their widening circle of foes had occurred on the homeward trek. The *baddies* were out there regrouping. She had no doubt.

Mato stopped the truck in front of the lodge, but left the engine running. He gazed ahead at the big stone and log building spangled with flurries in the headlights. "I'm having a moment. Gotta admit I wasn't sure we'd make it here in one piece."

"Or at all." Jackson's tone was somber. "If Don hadn't interceded for Morgan, I don't know where we'd be."

Her uncle grunted his acknowledgement of their appreciation. "As it turned out, she saved me. You all did. And there were plenty of iffy moments." He furrowed his brow at the lodge. "You think I'll be welcome here? Okema ordered me away."

"He banished the old you." Jackson laid a hand on his shoulder. "I'm alpha in his absence and invite the new Don to join us. Okema would approve. Just don't attack anyone over dinner. Grandma Miriam and Aunt Willow hate the mess."

"I'll bet." He grimaced. "I was hoping to put off any family brawls until tomorrow, or indefinitely. You might need to make the same suggestion to your father, uncle, and my sister. Maggie won't run to greet me after what I put her through. Sorry about that now."

Jackson smiled wryly. "As is she, being the one who bit you in the first place. You should've heard the angst. Come on. Let's get you inside."

Even with the curative drops, Uncle Don was a little weak. Rest was in order for everyone, but they had scant time for a much-needed break before the next round.

He nodded at Morgan. "Better help my niece out first. We don't want anything to befall the prize she's got."

After all she'd done today, the wind flying, battling vampires, and her ascension to the spaceship, having Jackson open the door for her seemed absurd. But she stepped from the truck with his assistance. No point in risking a tumble now. Better to get the egg safely inside.

Jimmy hovered at her elbow. "I'll take it from here, mighty leader. Get Uncle Don." He peered through his glasses at her snuggled bundle. The luminous shell shone through the filmy fabric in the darkness. "I can't wait for you to unwrap it, so I can get a good look."

She patted her gift. "It's unlike any egg in this world."

"Duh. Any in the galaxy."

"I guess so." She trod carefully on the snowy path, with him guiding her as if she were one hundred and ten years old. "I'm glad you're psyched about it, because I have no idea what to do with this thing."

"*Dragon*. Not thing. Didn't that turtle dude say to cook it in the hearth? You know, like *chestnuts roasting on an open fire*?" Jimmy hummed the tune.

She envisioned Ahmose's amusement at his comparison. "Not those exact words, but the general idea. Speaking of roasted nuts, the space drink wore off and supper's long past due."

"Jeeze, Morgan. You had snacks in the truck. I even gave you the last of my trail mix." He'd treated her like an expectant mother.

"Most kind. But not enough to satisfy the inner wolf."

Batboy guided her up the steps. "Hold on a little longer. Food is coming."

He spoke as if she were simpleminded. "I'd smack you if I weren't holding this egg."

The crunch of tires on the snow distracted her. Rafe and Hawthorne pulled in. Rafe cut off Big Blue's engine, and the two sprang from the truck. "Starving!" they shouted in unison, and tore up the steps.

"Hold up, Rafe. Baby on board." Hawthorne checked himself, and didn't rush past Morgan as he might've done in his 'All's fair in food and war' motto. "Don't want to jostle junior. I see Cubbie's got you both in hand."

"You think?" Jimmy sounded put out. "How often does a Star Person give us a dragon egg?"

"I got one last week. Didn't think to mention it." Impossible to suppress Hawthorne's high spirits for long.

Rafe chuckled. "I'm all about the egg, guys, just glad we're not overnighting in the forest. Figured we'd be there until the morning, or longer."

"I was afraid we'd be there the week." Jackson walked up behind them with Uncle Don on his arm.

Some of his lingering disability was due to the length of time that passed before she'd administered the drops. It was a miracle they'd saved him. All he needed now was food and rest.

The front door swung open. Miriam, Willow, and Dilly stood framed in the candlelight. Smiles and outstretched arms greeted them, and tantalizing scents from the kitchen.

Miriam raised her hands in thankfulness. "Praise be, you're safely back." One glance at Morgan's bundle and she stood stock-still. "Good heavens. Is that what I think it is?"

She nodded. "From Ahmose and the council."

"Oh my." The wise woman seemed star-struck, then she came to herself. "What a time you've had. The egg's Odessian, Willow."

An inhalation of breath accompanied this revelation. Willow grasped her son for support. "So, the

Star People are truly back?"

Hawthorne patted her arm. "Sure are, and they've taken a real liking to Wolf Girl here."

"Who has? What are you all talking about?" Poor Dilly was light years behind.

Hawthorne hugged her. "I'll fill you in after I eat an entire cow."

"Do that. Only it's stew and cornbread. And Dilly baked a cake." Miriam circled a sheltering arm around Morgan. "Come through to the kitchen. We'll need to get that egg into the hearth. Yes. Yes. I know you're all famished. Give me a minute to see to this, and we'll have supper on the table."

"They've returned? Oh, good." Aunt M.'s voice broke off. She scowled at her brother. "Who let the dog in?"

Morgan smiled wearily. "Uncle Don's one of us now. He saved my life."

"And she saved mine. Can we let past grievances go, and settle ourselves somewhere for a civil exchange, please Maggie?"

"Civil? You?" She snorted, but considered her twin with a quizzical air, a spark of hope in blue eyes identical to his.

The two siblings had been close once. Morgan prayed they would be again.

Jackson signaled Aunt M. "Take him to the main room, Maggie. You two have a lot to catch up on."

At their alpha's strong suggestion, she took her brother's arm. "Come on, then. I'll see if I can keep Peter and Buck from pulverizing you." The petite woman was a force to reckon with, now that she'd recovered from her ordeal.

"Rest, Don. We'll bring you a plate." Jackson walked with Miriam, Morgan, and the ever-present Jimmy. "He was bitten, Grandma. Morgan's got anti-venom for vamps, too, now."

"Does she, indeed?" Amazement underlay Miriam's soft reply.

Batboy bounced on his toes. "Yep. In a magic bottle in the space pouch she's wearing. How's Egbert?"

"Eating like a horse. He'll probably swallow one before long if we don't feed him enough. We need more hunters out getting deer, wild turkey, and rabbits for us and Egbert, but they have to watch their backs. And if the vampires are lethal, on top of their other powers…" her voice trailed off.

No words were needed to relay her undeniable dread.

Jackson closed his fingers around the sword at his side. "I killed one. Cut his head off. They're not invincible, just hard to beat."

Morgan couldn't agree more. "I ran through my blue energy battling Sitis. I'm sure not looking forward to encountering The Elder."

A shudder ran through Miriam. "Sitis and The Elder are here?"

"Somewhere," Jackson muttered. "Sitis got away, but Morgan beat him up pretty good."

Miriam's eyes wore a haunted look, like a long dead fear had returned. "Both are ancient and powerful vampires. Sitis means thirst in Latin. He's unquenchable, according to legend. The name, The Elder, speaks for itself. Neither has been in these ridges before. Only the younger ones. I didn't know how toxic their poison could be."

Good thing Morgan had heeded Radulf's advice and gone to the Divining Tree with Uncle Don instead of coming straight here. Miriam might not have been able to counter its effects.

Jackson clasped his grandmother's arm. "Don't worry. Who better to take out these bad boys than Morgan and me?"

"How about Egbert and Manetoh?" Jimmy exuded confidence. "Why does he have the same name as Okema?"

Miriam smoothed aside a strand of silver hair from her face. "It's the reverse, really. Okema Manetoh is named for him." She waved a hand at the surrounding walls. "Long before the lodge was built, before our people existed with the language we now speak, the Odessians were here. Manetoh is their name for the great serpent."

Jimmy pounced. "Only, he's a dragon."

She nodded. "Some believe there is a similarity between the two."

"Yeah." Morgan had wondered about that.

"Whether there is, or there isn't, the boy is right. Having a thunderbird and dragon, *properly trained,* on our side is quite a boon. We have much to be grateful for." Miriam sighed in satisfaction, also with what sounded like a tinge of regret. "I wish I could have been with Morgan and met Ahmose."

"You've heard stories of him, I guess?" She envisioned Native Americans seated around the campfire, swapping tales, over the centuries.

"Oh yes. He is the central Odessian with whom our people have spoken, on his rare visits. And he's our ancestor."

"Whoa." Jimmy swiveled his head at her. "You do realize he looks a lot like a turtle? Morgan said."

Holy crap. She was thinking the same thing. "But he mentioned he could alter his appearance. It's an Odessian talent."

Miriam's lips creased in a secret smile. "He can indeed, according to the accounts passed down to us."

Morgan stared at her. "What did he look like then?"

"A handsome young warrior, much like Jackson."

"Really?" She angled her head at him. "You're not, by any chance, an Odessian in disguise?"

Despite the long day, two days, or however many it had been, and everything that lay ahead, he chuckled. "You wish."

Jimmy slanted his eyes between them. "If she wasn't hugging the dragon egg, she'd punch you."

Jackson grinned. "I know."

Chapter Sixteen
The Gang's All Here

Waking up this morning was a challenge, even after Morgan dashed cold water in her face. Coffee, she needed coffee.

Still groggy, she navigated the stairs and headed up the hall. The murmur of voices and appetizing scents drew her. She stumbled into the kitchen to find Jackson's Uncle Ray and his sidekick, Dilly's warlock father, Joe, seated around the crowded breakfast table.

"Morgan!" Before she uttered a word, Ray leapt to his feet and engulfed her in a bear hug. Releasing her from the unexpected embrace, he beamed in never before seen exuberance. "Heard some amazing stuff about you, Number Seven."

The more reserved Joe tipped his blue hardware store cap. "Not that we're surprised. Way to rock it, Wolf Girl."

This tribute from an actual rocker wowed her. Well, as rocking as any member of their band, *Driving Nails,* could be. And they weren't half bad.

Both men's enthusiasm was a welcome boost and humbling at the same time. "Thanks, I mean, *megwich*, guys."

Jackson patted the empty seat beside him he'd evidently saved for her. "Join the powwow, Wonder Woman."

She smiled. "Thought you didn't go in for those?"

His lips curved in a dry smile, reflected in his dark eyes. "Call it a war planning summit, if you prefer."

She didn't. "Think I'll stick with powwow."

"Danger forever nips at our heels. Staying one step ahead of it is the key." He gestured at the group. "I figured why not breakfast and scheme in one?"

Joe saluted him. "That's why they pay you the big bucks, chief."

"Right." He snorted.

Morgan settled beside him and gazed at the gathering. They'd brought in extra chairs and stools. Those not seated at the long oak table were perched nearby.

She clapped her hands. "Hey! The fellowship's back together."

Jackson arched his brows at her, his lips twitching. "Yeah. I noted that too. Say, Dilly! Bring Morgan some coffee. She's in slowmo."

The girl flashed him a smile. "Just a sec."

Not only did they have the original fellowship back, but Miriam, Willow, Aunt M., and Dilly were busy serving fragrant plates of pancakes, bacon, eggs, and steaming mugs of coffee. Jimmy must've already eaten. He crouched at the corner of the hearth in the women's way, absorbed in the lustrous egg. Was it her imagination, or had it turned a deeper blue?

Low laughter from Hawthorne and the gathering recaptured her attention. Having this many together in one room was amazing. Even Peter and Buck had taken time off from their pressing work and battle preparations to join the throng. Uncle Don had been included, and no one was growling at him. Whether they had before her arrival, she didn't know, but sensed no undercurrent of hostility. His addition meant every living Morcant she was aware of had joined the Wapicoli. This, in itself, was historic.

Only Okema was missing from the group—a mega gap. Despite the crush, his chair at the head of the table remained vacant. Jackson had refused to occupy it until the chief was officially proclaimed dead. Even with Okema's absence, having everyone else assembled was huge. Sure, other Wapicoli lived in the ridges, but the clan only gathered on special occasions. The core of the hub was present.

Scent registered as keenly to a wolf girl as sight and sound; a meld of fragrances enveloped her, from the savory breakfast to the earthy note of Wapicoli males. Jackson's masculinity drew her like an intoxicating pheromone, and she inhaled the familiar mix of friends and family. Pride welled in her. She belonged to the most mind-blowing group in the entire galaxy. She wanted to embrace them all. Divergent emotions tore at her, joy at being a part of this awesome pack, when she'd never been a part of anything before, and fear of what might befall them.

"Here you go." Dilly plunked a plateful of delicious smelling food before her, and stuck a steaming mug in her hand.

"Thanks, Dill. You're a lifesaver." She took several much-needed swallows of the wakeup brew, laced with milk and sugar. "*Umm*. This is the stuff."

Maybe the coffee would clear her head and help her focus. The gathering had rather overwhelmed her with sentiment, and she swiped at her eyes. Aunt M. would probably tell her she was overtired, and that would also be true. There were those times in life, though, when you looked around and really saw the people dear to you, and embraced the fleeting moment. This memory would forever be etched in her mind.

Several more sips, and she realized the group must've been waiting for her to get settled before they began. Jackson rapped on the table, and the assembly quieted. Faces turned toward him with an expectant demeanor.

Was he making an announcement? They weren't officially engaged yet. Wait—war meeting. She needed more coffee.

He set his mug down and leveled his gaze at her. "Morgan and I are leading the clan together until Okema's return."

Eyes widened, including hers. "We are?" Weren't there tribal dictates for such matters? She was a relative outsider. "But he left you in charge."

He surveyed her in bemusement. "You still don't realize how essential you are to our survival. No one is more gifted, and the Star People have shown particular favor to you."

"Ahmose did call me Daughter of the Wolf and Stars, but he's very impressed with you, too, Jackson."

Mato lifted both hands. "As are we all, but you rule, Morgan. No offense, bro," he hastened to add.

Jackson shrugged. "None taken."

Hawthorne gave her a thumb's up. "What Mato said, just don't let it go to your head, Morgan."

Warmth flushed her cheeks. "Like I ever would."

Rafe pumped his fist in the air. "She's unbelievable. I saw her fly over a ridge, and up to the freakin' spaceship."

"Technically, it was a tractor beam—"

He brushed aside her attempt. "None of us could've done it, and then sailed back down without smashing on the ground."

Ray stabbed his finger at her. "More importantly, none of us were invited to try. They chose you."

Joe tossed his cap in the air, catching it before upsetting Ray's coffee. "Darn right, and that matters, girl."

"It sure does." Uncle Don's eyes shone like sunlight on lake water.

Dilly flipped her red ponytail. "Don't know why y'all are so surprised. I always said she was cool."

"Totally." Jimmy only spared Morgan a second with the wondrous egg roasting before him.

Seriously, it was bluer.

Aunt M. startled her with a high-five. "You've done far more than I ever thought possible, and I knew you had serious potential. I mean scary powerful stuff. I used to worry—"

"That's great." Morgan cut her off before they were treated to a recital of her nightmarish abilities. "But you've all witnessed me in action, or are close family members. What about the rest of you? Do you want me as a co-chief?"

Arms crossed over their leather vests, Peter and Buck studied her like a bug under a microscope. Jackson's gruff father hadn't exactly been a fan, but his stoniness had softened since Aunt M.'s arrival. And he'd given her grudging approval. Hawthorne's father, Buck, had never rebuffed her, but this was asking a lot of sticklers for tradition.

Peter shrugged a nod. "Dark times call for unusual

leadership. You're already a tested warrior. I say okay."

Buck grunted in agreement.

She looked to Miriam. Flames from the hearth played over her long silver hair and beaded, feathered earrings, and her brown eyes glowed. "Oh, yes. I told Okema you were the one."

Profoundly stirring. Still, Morgan had to ask. "What did he say in return?"

Her expression was solemn. "That you would save or destroy us, but must be given the chance."

"Yeah. He said something similar to me too." The lump in her throat made speaking difficult. "I vow to do my uttermost to preserve those whom I've come to love."

Jackson squeezed her hand. "Good. That's settled. If one of us falls, the other remains to lead."

"One of us shall." Morgan owed them the truth, and swept her hand at the gathering. "In this band."

He swiveled his head toward her. "What?"

"Ahmose said someone dear to me would fall." She lifted the *cartouche* from beneath her jacket. "This opens a portal in the Divining Tree. Whoever it is must be sent through the portal to Odessa. Only there, can healing be given."

Silence washed over the room. They must all be wondering the same thing she was. Who would it be?

Jackson weighed her revelation. "Can anyone other than you use this *cartouche* and gain entry to the sacred tree?"

An inner voice told her the answer. "No. I must open the portal."

He gave a low whistle. "Then we'd better hope you're on hand."

Assurance filled her. "I will be."

"How can you be certain?"

"I sense it will happen during the battle. I just don't know to whom." She ran her gaze over the faces fixed on her. "Anyone not fighting ought to be safe."

Miriam stirred from the near trance she seemed to have fallen into. "Are you sure?"

When it came right down to it, she couldn't swear this was the way events would play out. "No."

"What if the lodge comes under attack?" Miriam swirled her fingers in a loop. "I'll redo the protective charm straight after breakfast, and pray it's enough."

Uneasiness gnawed at Morgan. "To keep out Sitis and The Elder? Who can say? And what if Mateo and his gang make it through the barrier?" She shook her head. "I say we take the battle to the tree."

Jackson gaped at her, as did everyone else, except Jimmy. He straightened from his crouch by the hearth. "That makes sense. Lead them away from the lodge to the clearing, with those space dudes overhead, and the portal in range." Batboy shrugged as if it were a no-brainer.

"But no one is to view the sacred circle." Jackson's rebuke was reflected in the surrounding frowns.

Dilly plunked down a fresh cup of coffee in front of him. "What circle?"

He flung up a hand. "There. You see? We haven't even told her yet."

Joe puffed out his mustache. "I'm not up to speed either. But if I'm gonna fight in this battle, you might want to give me a heads up on where it's being held."

Jackson pressed his fingertips to his forehead. "It's not a road rally."

"Hold on." Mato waved the group to attention. "We don't normally get to determine where battles take place. They just sort of happen. Morgan may be onto something here. Why not devise a plan so we fight where it's to our benefit?"

"It's been known historically." Uncle Don rubbed his clean-shaven chin. "Brilliant military commanders have done the same." The studious librarian in him was showing.

Judging by Jackson's pensive expression, he was considering the proposition. They all were. He gestured at the bearwalker. "I don't know how brilliant this is, but go on."

Mato parted lips pursed in concentration. "You say the Panteras are counting on the Panther Moon to give them an advantage, which means they're plotting some kind of attack tomorrow evening. What if we choose where and move the event forward a night? Otherwise, a lot of you will be battling as wolves."

Hawthorne rolled his eyes. "What are we gonna do? Send out invitations, or shoot up some flares?"

"Sparklers worked for me," Jimmy reminded them.

"Why not bang a drum and sound the trumpets?" Jackson shook his head. "Not very stealthy."

Jimmy wasn't the least bit daunted. "It could be, if you're not in sight when the fireworks go off."

Batboy was a genius. Morgan saw the same revelation transform Jackson's sardonic gaze.

"You mean, draw our foes to the clearing, and then fall on them? Brilliant, Jimbo." He smiled. "Give the kid a medal."

No wonder Ahmose had praised him.

"It's not like the Panteras, or anyone else, know the

tree's anything special, anyway," Jimmy added.

Dilly flounced to the sink. "I sure didn't."

Newfound energy charged the gathering. Eyes brightened, heads nodded, and a buzz hummed through the group.

Jackson thumped on the table for silence. "Okay. What have we got? Hawth, you and Jimbo get a display together. Use whatever comes to hand. The rest of us will take stock of our weapons, and devise strategy. As much as we can. We tend to improvise." He flicked Morgan a wink. "A lot."

He turned to Jimmy. "One minor detail, Jimbo. How are we setting off the display if we're not there? Running a wire for dynamite?"

"Nothing that dramatic. I'm little and quick. I'll do it, then bolt for cover."

"I see." Jackson exchanged glances with Morgan. "I think he can pull it off. How about you?"

She hesitated. "As long as he's not the one I have to send through the portal."

The kid shrugged. "I'd get to visit Odessa."

"Ahmose didn't say it was a two-way ticket." And this worried her the most, along with the near-death thing.

Everyone in the room sobered.

Jackson wound his fingers through hers. "Maybe you ought to ask him, next time you two chat."

"He didn't exactly specify when that would be either. But I promise, whoever goes, I'll find a way to get you back." If that person was Jackson, she'd leap through the portal with him.

Joe cleared his throat. "I'll do it. We sometimes have special effects, pyrotechnic stuff, when we perform. Not like the big bands. But impressive enough for the crowd we draw. And I'm the one who sets it up. I've got a couple of boxes of stuff in my truck. And no one can move faster than a teleporter. Not even Jimmy here."

Jackson dipped his head. "You're right. Okay. New plan. Joe's heading up the display party."

"Want any help setting up and lighting it, Dad?" Dilly rested her hand on Joe's shoulder, a first between them.

His eyes reflected his pleasure at the gesture. "What do you think, Jackson? Two teleporters are better than one."

He grinned, heightening his appeal. "I say, bring it on."

Morgan squeezed his warm fingers. "And so say all of us."

His freckled face scrunched in concentration, Jimmy signaled for their attention. "Moving the battle ahead a night has gotta work. Morgan can't heave anyone through the portal, or use that *cartouche,* if she's wolfed out."

She shook her head. "I won't be."

Jackson eyed her as if she were delusional. "The Panther Moon's not just for Panteras gaining more power, you know. You'll change with the rest of us."

"Not all the way. Only partly, so I can draw on the wolf while retaining enough of my human self to better perform."

He made an impatient sound. "One full moon transformation nearly killed you, and now you've got this kind of control?"

"After what I went through with *Wandering Wolf,* I

learned a heck of a lot about control." And they all remembered that ordeal. "Maybe I'm wrong, but I believe I can do this. So can you, if you put your mind to it."

Exasperation hazed his eyes. "How, pray tell, when only Okema has ever resisted the pull of Sister Moon?"

She clasped his strong shoulder. "Draw deeply within yourself and find the gift you've been given. It's there. I feel it. I know it. You just have to believe in yourself."

His lips turned down. "Back to that, are we? Trying to make me like you."

"No. Simply encouraging you to be all you are."

Conflicting emotions flitted across his face like clouds chased by the wind. "I hope you're right about me, and yourself. The Panther Moon begins its draw early before reaching complete fullness. Tonight will challenge many of us with the call of the wolf."

She raised her chin. "Then I'll tell you what you're always telling me. Better power up."

Cheers broke out in the room. Members of the fellowship clapped and pumped their fists. Uncle Don and Aunt M. regarded her with glowing pride. Approval lit Peter's gaze, and it wasn't grudging.

Miriam smiled. "Listen to her, Grandson. She speaks the truth."

Jimmy perched behind him. "If you don't, she's liable to smack you. Besides, if you two fall apart, I'm taking charge of the *cartouche* and hoping Ahmose likes me as much as Morgan says he does. Cause y'all are gonna be wolves. No fingers. No thumbs."

A sobering thought.

Chapter Seventeen
Prepare and Beware

Even the birds were battered by the breeze blowing fresh Arctic air over Morgan and everyone else assembling in the yard. At least the snow had cleared out. Blue mid-afternoon sky peeked between the white boughs surrounding the lodge.

She eyed her brother huddled beside her in his charmed coat—re-charmed, actually. Miriam redid the protection spell. "*Invigorating* is one word for this icy blast. Are you warm enough?"

He stamped his boots. "I'll be Okay. I'm wearing layers beneath my *bunny* coat. Guess you don't mind the wind so much now." He flapped his arms suggestively.

"Flying has its uses. But I'd prefer a blazing hearth and toasting marshmallows to battle." Given their circumstances, the likelihood she'd need to harness the wind was high.

After refueling with sandwiches and hot chocolate, she and the others were heading back to the clearing. She nudged her fur-encased brother. "I suppose you packed extra snacks?"

"Extra everything. *Always be prepared*—the Boy Scout motto."

"Right." Batboy was seriously prepared for anything.

Jackson tried to be. He'd spent the day overseeing preparations on every front, and insisted she rest up for the big eve. "I felt totally lame lying around while everyone else worked."

"Naw. You're our secret weapon." Jimmy's eyes lit up. "Just wait until you explode like a bull from its pen in the bull riding ring."

She smiled. "Toss 'em high and drop 'em low, huh?"

"Whatever it takes." Judging by the jut of his jaw, Batboy was in earnest.

"All set!" Jackson heaved an armload of quivers with arrows into the back of Mato's truck. Fireworks, and whatever else Joe, Hawthorne, Jimmy, and Dilly had put together, filled the three vehicles. He surveyed the assembly from beneath his chestnut-brown fedora. "Is this it? Are we locked and loaded? For a group without firearms, I mean?"

Joe snapped him a salute. "*Red Leader's* ready, Captain."

Hawthorne smiled. "*Gold Leader's* packing."

Humor warmed Rafe's eyes. "Big time."

Jimmy frowned at them. "How come you get to be *Gold Leader*? You're in a blue truck."

"They called dibs." Mato patted his rusty orange pickup, dinged from yesterday's bullets. "We're ready to roll."

Jackson waved at the extra quivers of arrows tipped in poison for the warriors meeting them at the tree. "Grandma Miriam doesn't know what effect her concoction of nightshade, wolfsbane, hemlock, and mountain ash will have on Sitis, or The Elder, if they appear. Vamps exude their own poison, so they may be

151

immune. We're sure not, but she upped the potency with *three* deadly herbs plus the dark forces repellent."

Mato pulled the hood of his green canvas coat over the red bandana he wore twisted into a headband. "Don't shoot anyone you don't intend to kill. And don't miss."

The poisonous tips would inflict lethal damage on most everyone else, including themselves—a grave awareness they carried with them. They hadn't tested the antidote Ahmose gave Morgan to see if it worked on this potentially fatal brew. How could they? No volunteers.

Morgan gestured for attention. "Miriam will attempt to treat any warrior or ally suffering from accidental poisoning, but would rather not have to try. Strikes from *friendly fire* are strongly discouraged."

Jackson dipped his head. "It's a risky move using poisonous arrows. Remember our mantra, 'If in doubt, don't', doubly important given the Mountain Panteras are now our allies." He glanced at Don. "Heads up. They're the orangey-gold panthers when they shift. Mateo and his gang are the black ones."

"Good of them to be color-coded. Makes it easier for us," Uncle Don remarked drily.

Jackson shrugged. "We don't know if the difference between them has anything to do with the city Panteras separation from the mountains and treasure, or if they were always this way, and at odds from the beginning."

"Pirates aren't known for their ability to get along. Why are any of these Panteras our allies, again?" His blue gaze narrowed. "They killed my older brother, Jake, and sister-in-law, Susanna—Morgan and Jimmy's parents."

Hearing her mom and dad's names gave Morgan a start. Uncle Don and aunt M. rarely spoke them aloud.

Jackson brushed back lengths of hair escaping his ponytail. "Panteras also killed much loved members of my family, plus other Wapicoli kindred, but Morgan got Santiago and the Mountain Panteras to side with us. Wasn't easy. But we can't fight the whole world alone."

His father, Peter, nodded beneath a black cowboy hat. "Allies are essential in these dark days. We've sent Santiago an invitation to take part tonight." He frowned at the pickups. "Three trucks kind of make a convoy."

Ray clamped his camo-cap on more tightly in a gust. "I think we can count on getting noticed."

"Too noticed," Peter muttered, with a grunt from Buck. "Some of us should go by foot."

Jackson lifted conciliatory hands. "Roan, Sam, and other warriors are hiking over. We're the only ones driving. Santiago and his men won't give themselves away. We've got to get into position and may also need to make a speedy exit, with room for others to pile in. The newest member of our pack has an idea to confuse our enemy and lessen the odds of an ambush *en route*." He motioned at Uncle Don. "Tell them."

"One word. Decoy." Her remarkably recovered relation pointed at the two four wheelers, each big enough to carry two riders. He must've peeled off their snowy tarps, probably changed the oil, checked the tires, and given them a tune up while he was at it. He loved engines.

"I'll take one of these and whoever wants to ride with me. We'll go off-road by trail to the clearing, and make a few loops on our way." He smiled. "Our shenanigans ought to confuse the curious. Who's with me?"

Jimmy pounced. "I am. I have my bow and arrows, paintball rifle, and stuff. Tossing some sparklers here and there will add to the chaos. And I've got smoke bombs." Unbelievable what Batboy squeezed into his pack and pockets.

"Just the one I had in mind." Their uncle's welcome meant the world to Jimmy, judging by his gratified expression.

"Wait." Morgan couldn't let them head off without her. "I haven't handled a four wheeler before, but I call shotgun if someone wants to navigate the second one."

Uncle Don shook her hand. "Glad to have your support. Guess if we run into trouble, you can fly away."

She tilted her chin. "I'd never leave you."

He nodded his hooded parka. "I know. I've seen you fight."

The light in Jackson's gaze promised her she wasn't going alone. "I'll drive you."

"What the—I wanted to—" Hawthorne sputtered.

He intercepted his cousin's protest. "Another time, Hawth. Hightail it to the clearing. Joe can shield his truck with a spell, so it'll barely show. The rest of you keep a sharp watch out. Especially near the site. Direct newcomers into position and be ready to attack. Joe and Dilly will pop back and forth setting up the display. As soon as it's dark, they're lighting it. That's only a few hours from now."

Joe whistled through his teeth. "Gonna be quite the party."

Giving a snort, Ray thumbed at his comrade in hardware, rock music, and arms. "If the woods weren't dampened down with snow, he'd catch them on fire in this wind."

The touchy Joe bristled. "Not planning an inferno, Ray. Kind of defeats the purpose."

Dilly smiled. "It'll be great. Like the 4th of July, only super cold."

Jackson pursed his lips, then parted them. "We're not putting on a show for fun. This is serious battle stuff."

She tossed her head. Auburn hair, escaping the blue parka whipped across her face. "I know, but we might as well enjoy ourselves. No law against it, is there?"

"Probably half a dozen. Don't get me started on laws and permits, and the days when this was *our land*." He glared at his boots, then lifted his gaze. "By the time any government agents show up—if they do—we'll be in the thick of battle, or gone. If they don't make it out alive. Oh, well." He shrugged. "Protect innocent hikers who wander into the danger zone. The cold should discourage them."

Everyone nodded. They all seemed to share Okema's low opinion of government officials. Morgan was secretly shocked. Some of those agents had helped her and Jimmy in the Witness Protection Program, but she guessed she hadn't had to deal with what the Wapicoli had to remain undetected. They'd probably been more harassed than she realized, not to mention driven from their land, apart from this hidden remnant who'd hung on.

Jimmy waved at Jackson. "Before we go, can we

do the hand thing, like before a game?"

The annoyed lines in his face smoothed out. "Sure. Bring it in, guys. You first, Jimbo."

Boots crunching on the crusted snow, Batboy walked to the center of the gathering and extended his small gloved hand. Hawth went next. He stood next to Jimmy and laid his hand, palm down, over the kid's. Dilly covered Hawth's with hers and motioned to Joe. He added his hand to the rising mound. The circle widened with Mato, then Rafe, and Ray. Buck and Peter raised the level higher. Jackson signaled Don, who covered Peter's hand, then Morgan pressed her palm over the top of her uncle's. Last of all, Jackson completed the layer of hands and the circle, appropriate as the alpha.

He bowed his head, and everyone did the same. "Kiji Manitou, Great Spirit, we petition your blessing. Aid us in our battle and give us victory over our enemies this night."

Joe's gruff 'Amen' seemed fitting. Whether it was tribally appropriate, she had no idea.

"Go team." Jimmy's addition didn't surprise her. From the corner of her eyes, she glimpsed Jackson's faint smile.

He clasped Jimmy's shoulder with his free hand. "You're right. A pack is a team. We each do our part and fight for all we're worth. Not just for ourselves, for the world. We're entrusted with halting the darkness in our corner before it spreads. Others battle to do the same in theirs, and in galaxies across the universe. Mere mortals will never know of the dangers faced, or sacrifices made, on their behalf, but that doesn't matter. We fight as long as one of us lives."

"And if we all die?" Jimmy asked, in a small voice.

"Then humankind will perish." Jackson's reply had no edge of doubt. "Now, go. And may Kiji Manitou go with us."

Morgan's throat thickened and her eyes filled. He might not have the same gifts she did, but he was one heck of a leader. She couldn't have given such a stirring speech. Okema chose wisely when he left his grandson in charge.

A tightening clasp of their hands, then everyone dropped them to their sides as if in unspoken agreement. The group sprang to action, the guys and Dilly bolting for the trucks.

No time to linger over sentiment. Jackson grasped her fingers and they ran to the four wheelers with Jimmy and Uncle Don. She climbed behind Jackson and closed her arms around his waist. Engines revved. Trucks drove toward the road, and the four wheelers headed out. Jackson took the lead. He was the most familiar with the snowy track through the trees.

The four in their party each had a bow and arrows. She wore her weaponized scarf and carried a long knife. The men had tomahawks and knives. Jackson, alone, had a sword. Hers wasn't yet forged. Heaven only knew what Jimmy had brought besides the obvious.

These were only their outer weapons. They'd joined their vibrant spirits in an unbreakable bond with the pack, and they were werewolves. Their alpha descended from Ahmose, and was destined to be the next great white wolf. And she, well, she was the Seventh Morcant, with a brilliant brother, and genius uncle rescued from madness. Those who opposed them should beware.

Holding onto Jackson, she jounced on the seat behind him. Trunks and snow-covered brush whizzed by. She hoped they didn't hit a fallen log. "What if we run into something?"

"We keep the trail clear, and I know where the rocks are." He spoke over his shoulder, his voice muffled by the wind. "That's not what bothers me."

"What else?" she asked. "Apart from the battle looming over us?"

"I'm wondering if I ought to say any final farewells."

"Not feeling overly optimistic about this evening, are you?" She wasn't either.

"Maybe they'll patch me up in Odessa," he muttered.

A chill crawled down her spine. "Why are you so certain you're the one who'll fall? It could be anyone."

"Sure could. Not much of a morale boost either."

"No." She held tightly to him. "All we can do is our best, and I'll be ready for whoever it is. That person cannot be you, Jackson. We couldn't go on. I definitely couldn't."

"You think I'd cope better without you? Being a bold leader has its challenges. One day, I'm the seventeen-year-old understudy to the irreplaceable Okema. The next, I'm the big guy. We don't even know where he's gone." The hollowness in Jackson's voice when they'd first learned of Okema's disappearance reasserted itself.

"I know it's been rough—"

Snow flew up as he tore ahead. "You don't really get it, with your blue energy and flying, while I'm scrambling to preserve and protect. And figure stuff out, like war."

"I'm awed by you." If only he could know to his core how she felt about him. "You're brave, strong, handsome and—Eve."

"What—where?" He slowed.

She pointed. "There. With three of her pack."

The coyote witch wasn't whirling in dirt devils like she had before. She appeared in a puff of wind at the side of the trail, giving off a whiff of gardenia. White-blond hair tossed beneath a brown cap the same shade as her elegant leather coat and high boots.

"Always styling," Morgan muttered, "Ought to be a super model."

"Yeah. Guess we better deal with her." He paused the four wheeler and left the engine idling.

Uncle Don did the same behind them. Morgan better warn him. "Don't look *witchiepoo* in the eyes, Uncle."

Eve glared at her. "*Witchiepoo*? Seriously, *Morgan le Fay*?"

The comparison to the famous, albeit evil, enchantress, wasn't all bad. "I'll take it. Seen any vampires lately?"

Her pale lips curled. "Only slowpokes see them. We move too fast for vamps to keep up with."

Morgan shook her head. "You've just been lucky so far. What do you want, Eve?"

A wicked smile curved her mouth and glinted in her blue eyes. "You. Then Dilly."

"Not gonna happen." She zapped a ray of blue energy at Eve and sent her flying backward in the snow.

"Save your power." Jackson had an arrow on the string.

Pop. Pop. Pop. Pop. Jimmy blasted Eve and her peers with the garish yellow paint. This made four marked and mad coyotes. Shouldering his rifle, he grabbed his bow. Uncle Don already had the string taut and an arrow ready.

Sputtering fury, Eve rose to her feet, brushing off snow. She drew herself up as if to lunge at Morgan.

"Stop there," Jackson warned. "If any of us sends an arrow into you, you're dead, and it won't be a pleasant death. Don't make me shoot you, Eve. I've known you since we were kids."

She couldn't have appeared angrier if she'd spit, and held something in her hand. "Don't get sappy on me, Jackson. Better worry about your wolf girlfriend. If I hurl this into her, she'll die and it won't be a good way to go, either."

Recognition dawned, and with it a deep uneasiness. Eve held the fang from the sea serpent Morgan had talked the infuriated Mountain Pantera leader into parting with as a condition of their alliance, then passed to Lilith—the infamous barter to undo her spell on Jimmy.

Eve gloated. "It still has a drop of poison on the tip."

Morgan forced herself to remain calm, and not gaze into those gorgon-like blue eyes. "After all these centuries?"

"Want me to hurl it at you and find out?"

Jimmy aimed for her heart. "For Dilly's sake, cause for some reason, she cares about you, I'll give you one second to get out of here."

Jackson growled. "I won't even give you that."

Eve must've believed him. She whirled away so

fast they barely saw her leave in a yellow blur. Her fellow coyotes disappeared with her.

Relieved, but puzzled and alarmed, Morgan swiveled toward her uncle and brother. Jimmy was adjusting his bow, while their relation glared after the last spot they'd seen Eve.

He clenched the handlebar grips. "Where'd she get the fang? It looks ancient."

A shudder ran through Morgan. "Long story short, from her demon mother, who got it from me, who got it from Santiago. And it is ancient, possibly with venom unknown to us. Santiago kept the pointy end capped in silver. That's gone now."

Jackson's gold eyes burned. "If you see a giant lizard, Don, shoot her. Lilith Dubois has betrayed us."

"Big shocker there." Jimmy had voiced his plans for Lilith.

Uncle Don's sandy brows rose. "The Mountain Witch? I've heard of her. How does she come into this?"

"Eve and Dilly are her daughters, like the light and dark sides of the moon. Lilith put Eve up to this. She had to." Jackson radiated anger.

Morgan sensed which sister was ahead in this war, and it wasn't ditzy Dilly. "Lilith's got a plan. Always has. What a time for her to be carrying it out."

Jackson circled an arm around her and pressed his lips to her cold cheek. "Eve fled. We scared her off."

"For now." Morgan wasn't persuaded she'd stay away.

"If she returns, we shoot her full of arrows. No hesitation." Jackson drew a breath. "Meanwhile, we'll zig zag our way to the clearing. How about some smoke bombs, Jimbo?"

A chortle of glee from Batboy. "And sparklers?"

"Sure. I'll make a mystifying loop, in case we have spectators. Then head on. When we near our destination, we'll leave the four wheelers in the trees and walk the rest of the way. Unless, Morgan would rather fly?"

"Not unless I'm needed. I'll stay with you."

"Good." He smiled. "We'll steal through the woods and arrive in time for the show."

"A happier word for battle." She preferred to think of it this way.

"Much." Jackson took off again with Uncle Don on his tail, and Jimmy tossing smoke bombs and firing up sparklers.

Their efforts should buy the others time to arrive without unwanted attention, and get everything and everyone in position. If Mateo and his Panteras noticed the noisemakers—how could they not—they must be wondering *what the heck*?

Maybe they'd think the Wapicoli were celebrating some tribal holiday. When the fireworks went off, their enemies really would think they'd arrived fashionably late for the party. A great deal depended on the outcome of tonight's events. Probably even more than they knew.

Chapter Eighteen
Freaky Creepy

Fireworks whistled and starbursts exploded overhead, inflaming the skyline above the trees. If this smoky, multi-colored spectacle wasn't enough to attract attention, Joe had unleashed a recording of the greatest rock hits performed by *Driving Nails*. *Born to be Wild* played now. Good thing few people dwelled in these remote ridges, or they'd draw a crowd from miles around.

"Holy crap." Keeping her voice low, Morgan tucked next to Jackson, Jimmy, and Uncle Don hidden in shadows behind tree trunks. They were close enough to fall on curious Panteras if they showed, but far enough away not to be readily detected.

She exhaled in a breathy whistle. "This is a bold move, Jackson."

"Yeah." He closed his arm around her waist. "I'm a bold guy. Now, let's see how it plays out."

Uncle Don bent his head nearer hers. "It'll either be a glorious success, or a colossal failure."

"Guess you do what you gotta do to orchestrate a battle." She prayed they hadn't lost their collective minds. This had been a joint decision, but to see their scheme explode in living color, with music throbbing, was extreme.

Whew. She couldn't imagine Okema would've

sanctioned this in a million bazillion years. Too late to call it off now.

Jimmy *oohed* and *aahed* at the impressive display. "Better than a fife and drums any day, Jackson."

"Enjoy it while you can, Jimbo. Fifteen minutes is the span Joe and I agreed on, then we go dark with no trace we were ever here. He and Dilly will see to that."

Having teleporters in their pack sure was useful.

Morgan relaxed a little. "Fifteen minutes is too short a time for inquisitive folk to find us, unless one happens by."

"But X marks the spot for Panteras." The assurance in his hushed tone sent a prickling shiver down her neck.

She watched for the slightest movement in the trees not wind-related. "They may even show before the last song and flash in the sky."

"Anyone might." Uncle Don's warning ran through her racing mind.

The tug of the moon drew her like the tide, and she lifted her gaze to the nearly perfect orb rising through the branches. Only a tiny sliver was missing from the magical transition to full moon status, and the sphere's pull powerful. If this was to the Panteras' advantage, then it wasn't good for wolves.

"May we attend the gala, or have you someone particular in mind?" inquired a familiar, loathed voice from behind them.

She spun around, the shine of metal in the glow of fireworks catching her eye. Jackson had already drawn his sword. Uncle Don had an arrow on the string, and Jimmy leveled his paintball rifle at the intruder. Man, they were fast.

"Sitis." His name escaped her in a hiss.

Yellowish eyes shone in the face she'd come to detest, his purplish lips pinched in a smirk. "Even though you left me to die, I come in peace."

She wrinkled her nose at his blood musk scent. "Benevolent, considering you tried to kill me, and nearly succeeded in killing my uncle."

He shrugged, as if it couldn't be helped. "Yet, here stands Don Daniel. Before the boy blasts me, or I'm decapitated, or shot, I beg you to allow my companion a moment, *mademoiselle. S'il vous plaît.*" He waved his talons at the younger man who'd escaped her notice. The others seemed equally unprepared for the newcomer stepping beside Sitis.

Who the heck? Where had he come from? Miriam must be right, the more advanced vampires could teleport, or whatever they called appearing and disappearing.

She scrutinized the stranger with her keen wolf vision. He appeared totally unlike Sitis. Handsome, even. He wore a long black leather coat, partly open to reveal the fitted leather pants on his slim figure. Black boots reached partway to his knees. No hat covered his fair head. Only the telltale yellow in his eyes indicated he belonged to the blood suckers.

She might think the charismatic Spike had stepped from *Buffy the Vampire Slayer,* except this guy had longer hair and seemed less hardened. Not a badass.

Why on earth was he with the contemptible Sitis? Had he been bitten, turned into a vampire, and fallen in with the wrong crowd? Did the Guerriers constitute a crowd? Were there more of them nearby? Her thoughts spun wildly.

He held up a white ungloved hand, minus the talons adorning his companion's hideous fingers. "No need for alarm, Miss Daniel. We're here to parley." He exuded calm, his voice melodic.

Jackson didn't lower his sword an inch. "With whom do we have the pleasure of speaking?" Sarcasm underscored his tone.

Apparently, no offense was taken. A smile graced the speaker's pale face, enhancing his appeal. An aura of romance clung to his chiseled features, like a poet laboring too long over his jottings, in need of sunshine. This pallid complexion was the vampire in him, but the look also worked for an artist. She had a soft spot for artists.

He swept an elegant hand at himself. "I believe you have heard me referred to as The Elder."

"What?" She stared, openmouthed. He was the epitome of youthful male beauty. Nothing about him revolted her. Nothing in her wanted to attack him.

His eyes held particular fascination, and she found herself gazing into their depths. "You can't be. You're too—"

"Young?" he supplied, with a low laugh. "My dear girl, I've been around for a millennium."

Jimmy gripped his rifle. "Are you older than Ahmose?"

A flicker of annoyance crossed his mesmerizing gaze at the name. "No. Not that ancient."

Morgan jerked herself back to awareness. How easily she'd fallen under his spell. Better double her guard.

Tension tightening every muscle, she faced him. "What do you want, *Elder*?"

Again, the beguiling smile. "A treaty. We leave you and the Wapicoli alone. In return, you do not harass us."

Jackson growled. "So you can snack on whoever you like?"

The captivating eyes beckoned to Morgan. "What concern is that of yours, as long as our paths do not cross?"

She battled his almost irresistible draw, nearly as powerful as the moon's. "Last I heard, you wanted me to join you or die, so I'd say it involves me on a personal level."

He laughed softly. "From whom did you hear this? Sitis? You mustn't believe every word he utters. He exaggerates. Do you not, *mon ami*?"

"*Oui, monsieur*. A bad habit." The subservience transforming his loathsome face wasn't the Sitis she'd met.

Did he fear The Elder?

More explosions lit the sky and bursts of silver sparkled overhead. The musical accompaniment recorded by *Driving Nails* had switched to *Staying Alive*, an appropriate number.

There was more to this new vampire than immediately met the eye, and nearly impossible to wrench her focus away from his. Outwardly, he was the last thing she'd expected, charming, polished, and handsome in a romantic, soulful way. Did vampires even have souls?

His appearance, and what must be hidden beneath the outer façade, had to be polar opposites. But he was so darn good looking. And those eyes snared her at a glance.

Was she the only one falling victim to his charms? Were Jackson, Uncle Don, and Jimmy keeping him out of their heads?

"Morgan." Jackson's firm tone commanded her attention, before he addressed The Elder. "Apart from the threat issued to her, which you deny, are you seriously asking me, as head of the Wapicoli, to allow you squatting rights on our land?"

A rippling chuckle answered his charge. "You make us sound like homeless beggars. We are hardly paupers, I assure you. We have wealth and will purchase our own establishment."

"What, exactly, are you asking then?" Clearly, Jackson hadn't relaxed his guard.

The newcomer exuded ducal charm. "An assurance there will be no animosity toward us on your part. And we will leave you and yours alone."

"Werewolves don't taste good, huh?" This dry observation came from Uncle Don.

The Elder sniffed, as if at a disagreeable smell. Their pack, she supposed.

"We will also exclude any humans under your protection, such as this child." A suggestion lingered in his tone.

Jackson bristled. "Is that a threat?"

"Simply an observation. Not all of your people are wolves." He bent and inhaled Jimmy. "Some are divinely human. Ahhh. So sweet, this innocent." He lifted his head and smiled at Morgan, revealing a hint of fangs.

Was he implying Jimmy was on the menu, if they didn't cooperate? And Dilly, if he could catch her? And the Wapicoli women not inherently wolves, and whoever else they wanted?

Yes. That's exactly what he meant.

Heat crackled in her like fire in the stiff breeze. He didn't appear quite so beautiful anymore. In fact, she no longer liked his face one little bit. He'd hurled the gauntlet. By heaven, she was hurling it back.

Jimmy slid his gaze between them. "Someone's in trouble."

"Sure is." Jackson gestured her ahead.

Uncle Don looked on, his bow drawn.

Summoning her inner wolf, she fixed burning eyes on the watchful vamp. "I am the co-chief of this band, your highness, and I say no pact. Touch my brother and I'll tear you apart. Hell! I will anyway!"

Forget keeping her voice down. Forget the Panteras. If Mateo arrived before she was finished here, someone else could fight him. She was getting this beguiler.

Blue energy electrified her, and she flung her hand at him. Surprise touched his eyes as he reeled back.

Sitis leapt aside. "I warned you about her."

"But this?" The Elder waved his lilywhite fingers in her direction. "Astonishing."

Jimmy blasted him in the nose with his garish yellow trademark. "She gets worse."

"Much." Whirling upward in the wind, she spun at him, hurling blue fire with both hands.

He tumbled to the snowy ground, his fair hair smoking. She circled above him in a blue glow. Should she dive-bomb him now, or wait until he rose and blast him again?

Uncle Don shot an arrow at his heart.

He rolled to the side with the speed of *The Flash*,

and was on his feet in an instant.

Jackson raised his sword and rushed at him. "We're the guardians here. We say who stays and who goes. And you failed the test."

Before he got in a swing, The Elder vanished, and Sitis with him. Jackson lowered his blade. "Tough to lop off the dude's head when he won't stay put."

"Exceedingly." And Jackson was plenty fast himself. Morgan sailed back down to her feet. "I should have swooped in. Think I could have taken him."

"You?" He snorted. "Maybe after you came to your senses. He had you in the palm of his hand before that."

She squirmed at the memory of how easily he'd captivated her. "His mesmerizing powers were more than I'd bargained on, but you have to admit, he was far younger and better looking than we expected. All that charm was tough to deflect."

The three guys swiveled toward her in astonishment. Jackson sheathed his sword. "Are you kidding? He looked about a thousand. I wondered if you were dreaming when you said he was too young to be The Elder."

She was baffled. "But that's what I saw."

Jimmy shouldered his rifle. "He looked plenty old to me. Maybe he has the power to make you see what he wants."

"Yes." Uncle Don gestured at her. "As the only female among us, you were more susceptible to a younger, attractive man. So this is how he appeared to you."

She rearranged the weaponized scarf around her neck. "Wonder what he really looks like?"

"An exceedingly old man in a black hooded cloak."

Jackson waved at the others. "Agreed?"

Heads nodded. Uncle Don stood in a pensive posture, rubbing his chin. "Although, none of us may know for sure."

"So, you guys didn't see the tiniest resemblance to Spike?" As a hardcore *Buffy* fan, she had to ask.

"I'll bet he's a mind reader." Jackson slapped his hand on his side. "He saw what you wanted in your head and imitated it. I'm surprised he didn't sparkle like *Edward Cullen*."

"I'm more of a *Jacob Black* type."

"The wolf dude in *Twilight*?" He gave a short laugh. "I guess that would have been too obvious a choice for him to pull, even with you under his spell."

Jackson's words sank in. The Elder had focused on her. "Why is this about me?"

He grew somber. "You were always the target. He hardly spared the rest of us a glance."

Uncle Don clasped her shoulder. "The sly old guy was testing you."

Indignation flared in her. "Well, I wasn't going to let him make a meal of Jimmy."

"I wasn't going to let him either. Hello," Jimmy waved at her. "I'm wearing my bunny coat. Not that I don't appreciate you charging to my aid. You were awesome."

"Thanks." She took some satisfaction from his praise. "He's had a taste of what he's up against with me now."

Another taste, another time, Wolf Girl. The melodic voice whispered in her ear, and then he seemed to buzz past her.

She whipped around. "Where did he go?"

"He's not here." Jackson swept wary eyes over the trees. "No neon yellow blotch anywhere. Why?"

"I heard him." And it gave her the creeps. "Can he make himself invisible? I hate that stuff."

"I'm not a fan either—" Jackson began.

She broke in. "It makes me want to smack myself, like when a spider's crawling on me and I'm trying to get it off, and scream, and jump out of my clothes."

"Yep. She does." Batboy could bear witness.

"Over a spider? The girl who scorns vampires." Jackson shook his head, humor hinting at his mouth.

"Oh, the vamps are worse." Chills still shuddered through her.

Chapter Nineteen
Never Give Up

Smoke from the fireworks lingered in the cold bluster, but the show had concluded. The clearing was still. *Waiting*. Morgan, Jackson, Jimmy, and Uncle Don watched from behind the wide trunk. How many other warriors also looked on, she couldn't be sure. Their presence was undetectable.

Sniffing the air, Jackson gestured at the circle in the trees. "We've got company. Panteras. *These*, you can see, Morgan."

Thank heavens. Mateo and his gang weren't so bad compared to the disappearing—and reappearing—rattlesnake vampires.

She, Jimmy, and Uncle Don clustered by Jackson and peered at the clearing. Sure enough, a small gang of armed Panteras crept into the glade. She counted four.

"Scouts," he hissed. "More will follow."

The plan was to wait until as many as possible had gathered in the opening before taking fire. "Arrows on the string. You, too, Jimbo. Paint 'em later." Jackson barely breathed the words.

She readied an arrow. What she really wanted was to incinerate Mateo. If she seized his head between her hands, he was going up in blue flames. "Are we using the poisonous arrows? Seems a little harsh for the younger men."

"They're already killers." Jackson stabbed his finger at the converging gang. "Who are they, Morgan? Tell me."

"Our enemies." She matched her hushed tone to his.

"You want to win this battle?" His question didn't require an answer.

Hesitate and lose. This whispered advice hadn't come from Jackson.

Battling the shriek rising in her throat, she forced out a strangled, "I hear you."

Jackson glanced around. "Of course. I'm right here."

Tremors ran through her. "Not you. *Him.* The Elder."

"Whoa." Batboy pivoted in every direction. "He's nowhere in sight. Not even a yellow blur."

"Then how is he speaking in my ear?"

Uncle Don assumed his thoughtful air. "Voice projection is a possibility."

"Better than the creeped out feeling he's right beside me." Determination welled in her. "Next time. No hesitation. We go for the kill."

"Assuming we can be certain *who* he is, with his different guises." Jackson's eerie suspicion was already in her head.

He held a finger to his lips. More Panteras were arriving. The music and fireworks had died away while she lit into The Elder, but they'd answered the call.

A silent, but palpable, hum of expectation ran through the hidden warriors awaiting Jackson's signal. He motioned at the other three. "I'll fire first. Then you."

Positioning himself to the side of the trunk, he drew back the bow string, and shot the initial arrow. The shaft buried itself into the chest of a Pantera wearing leathers, a gold chain around his neck. He didn't even cry out, just toppled over. He didn't have to worry about the onset of poison. This guy wasn't getting up.

More arrows whizzed into the glade, Uncle Don, Jimmy, and Morgan's among them. Some felled their targets outright. Others struck legs and shoulders. Howls of pain and rage tore from the ambushed gang. Like wounded grizzly bears, they flew into furious action. And not all were injured. A volley of gunfire burst at the furtive warriors, tearing bark from the trees, and eliciting yelps.

Oh no. Some of the Wapicoli were hit.

Who? The anguished question hammered inside her. She prayed no one in her close-knit pack lay wounded. Or worse. Werewolves had phenomenal healing abilities, but none could recover from death. Nor could a bearwalker, warlock, or teen witch—

"Get down." Jackson tugged her to the base of the tree. "Our first flight of arrows was vital. Now, we can only risk guarded shots from cover."

Gunfire erupted around them. The staccato blasts ratcheted through her raw nerves. She wanted to curl in a ball with her hands over her ears.

Howls rose on the night wind. Wolves. The moon's pull was too strong for some to resist turning.

Jackson groaned under his breath. "We're screwed. We need every archer we have left. If wolves bound into the clearing, they don't always reason—just react. They'll get shot."

Thank heavens Uncle Don was holding out in human form, and Jimmy would keep firing. She steeled herself. "This is where I go in."

"Nothing doing." He closed his fingers around her wrist. "You're not bullet proof."

"The blue energy may be."

He shook his head. "We don't know that."

She had to make him see. "I've got to take the risk. They'll kill us all if I don't. Besides, it's tough to strike a swirling object."

Jimmy shouldered his rifle. "Morgan's right. She'll be on 'em so fast, they won't know what hit 'em. And I'll paint every last one."

"Don, what do you say?" Jackson appealed to him.

He considered. "I hate letting her go as much as you, but we don't have a lot of choice. And I believe she'll prevail."

"So do I, but she's Morgan. I can't bear to lose her." Jackson flung down his bow and caught her to him, wrapping her in his arms. "My sweet, fiery, amazing girl."

He pressed his lips over her cold cheeks and covered her mouth, kissing her with all the passion he'd pent up. He held nothing back. Never mind Jimmy and Uncle Don looked on. He showed her how much she meant to him, and she returned the fervent pressure on her mouth, kissing him as if it were their last, because it might well be.

They could delay no longer. After an infinitely precious moment between them, she broke their kiss. "It's what I'm meant to do. Why I'm here."

Deep down, he must realize the truth. She sensed the battle raging inside him.

He released her with acute reluctance. "Go, but take care. Mateo's not among the fallen or injured."

"I know." Those glittering tawny eyes were unmistakable.

Wolf howls rose louder. More warriors had turned. Armed Panteras would take a heavy toll if she didn't stop them.

Jackson squeezed her fingers. "Plough the field. We're right behind you."

"Stay under cover as long as you can. Don't any of you dare fall in the fight." Taking a final look at their dear faces, she circled upward in the wind.

This feat would take every ounce of power she possessed, and more. She summoned her inner light. Where her blue energy ended and the wolf began, she wasn't sure. The two seemed to go together, probably why Ahmose called her Daughter of the Wolf and Stars.

No need to rub the moonstone tonight. Maybe it was being near the Divining Tree, or the blessing from the Star People. Whatever the reason, energy freely flowed into her. Like flashes of lightning, she radiated blue as she swirled past branches, above the trees, and over the clearing.

Men stopped in their tracks, heads arched heavenward. Gunfire paused and they stood gaping at her. This stunned moment was her best opportunity to act.

Revolving like a cyclone, she flung blue rays at any man she saw. Singling out Mateo was impossible at this speed. Shocked Panteras cried out and hurtled to the ground, even flopping onto their sides. If they had any sense they'd stay down. Some struggled to rise. Others bolted.

Fire burned in her. Blue flames crackled from her fingertips. She unleashed a second round at them, scorching the very air.

Zap. "That's for my mother!" She flung another sizzling ray. "And my father!" Swirling in a volatile circle, she dispensed justice. "And that's for Jackson's mama!" A fling of her charged fingers. "And his grandfather!" Still spinning, she sent another flash at the scattering gang. "This is for the murdered kid and the kind recreation worker!"

"Morgan Daniel?" A defiant Pantera scrambled to his feet, his black hair standing on end.

Wait—he wore it spiky. *Mateo.*

Teeth outlined in gold glinted in his wicked smile. He didn't hesitate to fire at her, blistering the heavens.

None of his bullets hit their mark. She revolved like a skater in the flurrying finish of a grand performance. Only, she wasn't finished. His shots dinged off the blue glow as if they'd struck metal, and ricocheted into the moonlit sky.

Warriors loosed another barrage of arrows. Mateo remained unscathed. Thin high cries carried from the trees. Wolves were gathering.

Jimmy went to work. Any man left standing was plastered yellow, and some who were down, thrashing to rise.

Mateo whipped toward the spot where Jimmy hid. Batboy gave him a snootful. The incensed Pantera leader sprinted at the trunk where he, Uncle Don, and Jackson waited.

Fear seized her heart, and she circled lower. She'd be on Mateo before—

Panther shrieks tore from the trees. Orange-gold

mountain lions bounded into the clearing. Santiago and his Panteras were in the game. They rushed toward Mateo's shifting gang. Powerful cats slammed together in a clawing, biting clash. The spectacle was unlike anything Morgan had ever seen, or likely would again.

Mateo left the others to it. He aimed his rifle at Jimmy, Jackson, and Uncle Don's hideout and ran at them, firing as he went. Bullets ripped into the tree they'd ducked behind. Snow flew in puffs and chunks of bark sprayed out. They didn't dare stick a head around the side of the trunk to shoot an arrow. If Jackson or Uncle Don shifted and charged him, he'd shoot one or both before they'd flattened him to the ground.

Normally, Morgan would be low on energy by now and need to refuel. But enough power remained to defend her own. Swooping at Mateo like a dive-bomber, she flashed blue light and knocked him off balance. His bullets discharged harmlessly overhead.

The instant he hesitated, whistling arrows answered. He was shot. One. Two. Three times. Each of the guys must have sunk an arrow into him.

With a mighty howl, he yanked the shafts from his arm, leg, and side. The poison might take a little while to work, but he wasn't immune to its effects. Meanwhile, rage propelled him forward. He and his rifle were on the move again. Bullets flayed the trees. He'd kill them all!

She circled at him again. This time, she'd go for his head, and prayed she had enough sizzle left to finish the job. Before she reached Mateo, the largest, most brilliantly colored orange cougar hurtled at him.

The gang leader threw down his rifle and shifted

into a huge black panther. They tore into each other. 'Fighting like cats' took on a whole new, deadly meaning.

Was it Santiago paying Mateo back for hunting his men, and stealing their treasure?

No need for Morgan to incinerate him. He couldn't win. This would be Mateo's final battle. Miriam's lethal brew was setting in, weakening him. The opposing panther did the rest. A fitting end for the murderous gang leader, she supposed.

She touched down on the glade, her boots crunching snow. Orange and black Panteras were ripping into each other on every side. Wolves ran from the trees and joined the fray. Snarling, slashing, biting—bedlam. Jackson was in the thick of it, firing arrows. She spotted Hawthorne, Mato, and Rafe.

Uncle Don must've kept Jimmy under cover and out of the fight. Thank heavens. He might be wonder boy, but he was still a kid, probably annoyed at missing the battle. At least he'd gotten in one good shot to crow about. And she was finished, her aid no longer required. She'd done her part. Their side was winning.

Some of Mateo's gang raced toward the woods and a speedy getaway. They'd shift back into human form when they reached their cars. She predicted those injured by arrows would seek treatment at the nearest hospital for debilitating symptoms beyond their wounds. These might pull through, but most of the city Panteras were falling, or already down. History no one would believe was in the making, and the end of an evil gang.

A loud hurrah went up from those not in wolf or panther form. The victors claimed the field. Only the beaten remnant of Mateo's band had escaped.

Jackson ran toward her, triumph on his face. Their crazy scheme had worked.

"*Morgan Le Fay.*"

Only one person had called her by that name. She spun around. *Eve*.

Chapter Twenty
Vengeance and Victory

Blue eyes slitted with purpose, Eve stabbed the venomous serpent's tooth at Morgan's heart.

No escape. A moment frozen in time, scented with the overpowering fragrance of gardenia.

A brilliant flash, like streaking light, and Okema appeared between them. He must've powered up big time because she'd never seen him so radiant.

Instead of driving the fang into her intended victim, Eve plunged it into Okema's chest. Horror enveloped Morgan. Had it struck his heart, or entered slightly to the right? What difference did the entry point make if the vile tooth was as poisonous as they feared?

All this passed through her stricken senses in an instant.

He gave a faint gasp and shuddered. Like a towering tree, he swayed, then crumpled to the snowy ground.

Before she tore the fang from Eve's hand, Jackson was there. Rage twisted his face into an unrecognizable mask. Eve blinked in surprise when he turned the ancient weapon on her. The bloody point raked her side as she whirled away, leaving it and her glove in his hand. Red spattered the whiteness beneath them, dotting the snow here and there in her swift escape, the yellow blob from Jimmy's paint, a blur. If any poison remained in the long dead serpent's tooth, it now sped through her.

Morgan could spare no more thought for Eve.

"No! Not Okema." Crying his name, she sank to her knees beside him and cradled his head in her lap. The three golden feathers in his white hair fluttered in the breeze. A red stain marked the front of his buckskin coat.

The woodsy scent of the forest filled her senses, the essence of him. Wrong! This was wrong. It seemed as if the very earth should cry out.

Never in her wildest imaginings had she envisioned his falling could hit her this hard. He'd been the source of her family curse, of much suffering and sorrow. And yet, she'd grown to admire and care for this mysterious chief. In an inexplicable way, he'd become her grandfather, her mentor, and she, his protégé.

Tears streamed down her face. "I've failed you."

He stirred weakly. "No. You saved us."

"You saved me." The sob tore from her.

Jackson knelt beside her, blinking at the moisture filling his eyes. He smoothed the hair of his fallen kin with a trembling hand. "How can I lead without you, Okema?"

His lips moved slightly. "You already are."

How faint was his reply.

Uncle Don and Jimmy stood at their side. When had they arrived? Jimmy's eyes were grave. He worshipped this chief. Uncle Don wore an expression of profound respect.

Other warriors in human and wolf form gathered around the fallen leader, so powerful none thought he could be brought low. Their cries and howls lifted to the moon. Great was their agony, and wrenching to hear.

"Don't go, don't go," Morgan repeated to him, her tears wetting his ashen face. The injury alone hadn't wreaked this tragedy. Poison from the serpent was working fast.

She gazed at Jackson through the watery film. "He's fading." She could scarcely speak through her sobs.

"He means this much to you?"

Another shuddering cry shook her. "Yes."

A strange hope transfixed his grief-stricken gaze. "Don't you see? He's the one you're meant to send through the portal."

Everything grew clear to her. She must pull herself together and act quickly. "You're right. Help me. We've got to move him now."

"I'll do it." Jackson gently slid his arms beneath the beloved chief and bore him to the sacred tree.

Morgan hastened at his side. The band of warriors and Mountain Panteras followed behind. Their silence was overwhelming, except for howls from the wolves flanking them.

Jackson paused before the wide-spreading oak. "It's up to you now, Morgan."

Holding out the *cartouche* with one hand, she grasped the furrowed bark with her other, and lifted her eyes to the sky.

"Ahmose, hear me, this is the one dear to my heart who must come through. Please, I beg you, open the portal."

The moonstone hummed as if it picking up a signal, and a bright light shone from inside the tree.

Had it hidden a secret all these years?

An opening in the massive trunk took shape before them. Here was her invitation.

"Thank you!" Gasping her gratitude, she kissed Okema's brow. "You are going to Odessa to be healed. I swear you shall return to us."

"Your word is good, my wolf daughter." His voice was a faint whisper.

Pride mixed with her gut-wrenching emotion.

Jackson laid him inside the tree on the earth shining in the light. He knelt, clasping his limp hand. "*Tanakia*." He spoke the Shawnee farewell for 'until our paths cross again', then stood and closed an arm around Morgan.

While they watched Okema's limp form, a beam brighter than any she'd ever seen lifted him from sight. One moment he was there, and the next, he wasn't. This was far faster than her rise to the spaceship. He'd entered the portal and must be rushing through space. The shooting stars and falling moons Radulf had described would be lost on him in this state. Perhaps, he'd admire the cosmic wonders on his return trip.

With the chief's departure, the light in the tree went out and the opening closed. It was as if the door had never been. And who could say when it would open again?

She and Jackson stared at each other in numb disbelief. None of the stunned onlookers made a sound. Even the wolves ceased to howl. The Mountain Panteras seemed as shocked as anyone, perhaps more so.

Jackson stirred. He turned from the tree and faced those awaiting his leadership. "Okema has gone where the Star People will heal him. He shall return to us. Until then, I am your alpha. And Morgan Daniel is my co-chief and future mate." He spoke her name loud and proud, and a thrill ran through her.

Smiles brightened faces still stunned from sudden events, and dismay lifted from their eyes. Cheers broke out.

"I don't know if anyone noticed, but we won." Jimmy waved at the clearing. Fallen gang members, and orange and black panthers littered the ground.

Their victory had come at a cost. Jackson circled his gaze at the battlefield. "Did we lose any warriors?"

Mato shook his head. "No. We have wounded to get back to the lodge and Miriam's healing."

Jackson seemed to seek someone in particular. "What of Santiago?"

In answer to his query, the leader of pirate descent walked to him in cuffed leather boots. A red scarf emblazoned his head beneath the faded tricorn hat. He wore his dark brown hair loose over his leather coat. A tier of gold and ruby balls dangled from his ears. Scratches marred his face, and his gait was stiff, but he'd live.

"Our work here is done, leader of the Wapicoli. We will care for our own dead and wounded." He eyed Morgan with his keen black gaze. "Shall we continue our pact, Morgan Daniel?"

She held out her hand. "We shall. The Mountain Panteras remain our allies."

Santiago nodded and shook her hand, then turned to Jackson. "She speaks for you, as before?"

"She speaks for us all." He clasped the Pantera leader's outstretched fingers. "We will honor our side of the pact."

Jimmy tugged on Santiago's sleeve. "If you want your fang back, it's lying in the snow over there." He pointed.

"Thank you, small one." He beamed, no doubt gratified at the return of the relic he'd worn on a chain around his neck, a tribute to their days at sea.

Jackson stepped aside and gestured at the assembly. "Gather the injured into the trucks. Let's head back to the lodge. Those of us who arrived on four wheelers, will return on them."

He didn't appear excited at the prospect, and Morgan would prefer a more restful ride. The fight had drained her, and she longed for the lodge. Snowy roads were bad enough, without navigating trails at night.

Hawthorne shook his head beneath his fedora. "You guys ride in the pickups. Rafe, Mato, and I will take the four wheelers."

"Not leaving me out." Ray stood beside his son.

"And Ray." Likely, Hawth didn't care, as long as he commanded one of the vehicles.

Joe and Dilly materialized. Morgan reached out her hands to them. "Thanks for all you did. We couldn't have pulled this off without you."

Dilly pinkened with pleasure, and Joe smiled in his gruff way. Both gave her fingers a squeeze.

"Morgan Daniel?" The voice sounded official.

A uniformed man with a flashlight approached them. At a glance, he appeared to be a Park Ranger in his green jacket, pants, and wide-brimmed brown hat.

What on earth? Almost too shocked for words, which was saying a lot after all she'd experienced in the past twenty-four hours, she watched him near. "Yes?"

He shone the light in her face, eyeing her through his glasses. "I was passing, heard some commotion, so stopped to investigate. Witness Protection asked us to keep an eye out for two juveniles who disappeared not far from here over a month ago. We're following up on rumors that you and your brother, Jimmy, are still in these ridges."

"Yep." Jimmy waved at him.

He scanned the kid. "I'm supposed to get you two resettled in a new location for your safety. Is your aunt living? She's also missing."

Uncle Don stepped nearer. "She is, and I'm their uncle."

The ranger seemed satisfied, but puzzled.

How shocked he'd be if he knew what danger she and Jimmy had endured, and what peril he, himself, now faced.

Disapproving rumbles ran through the Wapicoli onlookers. Santiago didn't appear pleased, either. Neither band appreciated government interference of any sort.

Sidling uneasily, probably wishing he'd brought back up, the ranger shone his light at the group. "Who are you people?"

Morgan spoke first. "Friends. They've protected us."

His beam touched on some of the fallen. "Good Lord. What happened here?"

"Mateo." Speaking his name still sent dread through her. "He and his gang attacked in their search for Jimmy and me. There was quite a fight."

"Yeah. I heard." He sucked in a sharp breath. "They're not all gang members. Some look like—"

"Panthers?" she interjected. "Jimmy and I no longer need assistance from Witness Protection, sir. Mateo lies among the dead. There." She pointed at the immobile big black cat.

He directed the beam of light where she'd indicated. "Impossible. What are you on, girl? That's a panther. I've never seen so many panthers together in these woods. None that large. Ever."

She'd anticipated his response. "What about wolves?"

The light reflected on his glasses revealed his incredulousness. "They haven't been seen in these parts in ages. You must be scared out of your wits after the attack. You and the boy come with me. And your uncle, if he likes. As for the rest of you—" He frowned. "I don't know what's going on here, but I'll send the sheriff and deputies to sort this out. You need a permit to kill big cats, and some of those men are stuck full of arrows. You wouldn't by any chance be those Indians I've heard of? Wapi—something?"

Uh, oh. He was getting too nosy for comfort. If she didn't intervene, he wouldn't make it out alive. "Tell you what, you go back and report what you've seen here to whichever officers you like, and let us know what they say. Be sure and tell them about the panthers, and the werewolves."

As she uttered the final syllable, she shifted into a glossy white wolf and fixed her glowing blue eyes on him.

The flabbergasted man stared at her, opening and closing his mouth. No words came out.

All around him others were changing. Jackson, Hawthorne, and Rafe turned into large gray and tan wolves with gold and green eyes. Peter and Buck were black wolves with red eyes, and Santiago shifted into the large orange panther she'd seen before. Mato turned into a big brown bear. Rising on his back legs, he pawed the air, and opened his mouth in a roar. Howls, growls, and feline shrieks filled the clearing.

With a horrified yelp, the ranger pivoted on quaking legs and fled back the way he'd come. A jeep revved up. Tires crunched over the snow, and he peeled out of there. Somehow, she doubted he'd make that report. If he did, he'd be sent to a mental ward. When you report seeing something unbelievable, no one believes you. They think you're crazy.

In time, word of Mateo's death would circulate from the survivors of tonight's battle and reach Witness Protection. The search for her and Jimmy would cease. If and when they surfaced, the simple explanation that they'd hidden in the ridges for safety's sake would suffice. Aunt M. could plead the same, though Morgan expected she'd stay with the Wapicoli. As for Uncle Don, who knew? Perhaps, he'd reclaim the cabin, and maybe a few members of his pack could be persuaded to side with the Wapicoli.

She and Jimmy would remain in these woods and fulfill their destiny as guardians of the forest. The past no longer had any ties on them. She lifted her eyes to the stars. Somewhere, in a galaxy far away, Okema was being ministered to on Odessa.

The unfathomable chief had said something about her and Jackson fulfilling the prophecy. She met his golden gaze. Had they done so, or was there more to come?

He was not yet the great white wolf, and much lay

untapped between them. Lilith, and possibly Eve, and her coyotes were still threats. Not to forget Sitis, and the infinitely creepy Elder for a moment, plus the Guerriers.

Jackson wrapped her in his arms, and sweet warmth flowed through her. Intuition told her their adventures had just begun.

A word from the author...

Married to my high school sweetheart, I live on a farm in the Shenandoah Valley of Virginia with my human family and furbabies. An avid gardener, my love of herbs and heirloom plants figures into my work. The rich history of Virginia, the Native Americans, and the people who journeyed here from far beyond her borders are at the heart of my inspiration. I'm especially drawn to colonial America and the drama of the American Revolution. In addition to historical romance, I also write time travel, paranormal, YA fantasy romance, and nonfiction.

www.bethtrissel.com